ESCAPE FROM WARSAW

(formerly *The Silver Sword*)

By IAN SERRAILLIER

Illustrated by Erwin Hoffmann

SCHOLASTIC INC.

New York Toronto London Auckland Sydney

To Helen

"Here is no final grieving, but an abiding hope. The moving waters renew the earth. It is spring."

Michael Tippett, *A Child of Our Time*

ISBN 0-590-42534-X

Originally published by Jonathan Cape Ltd., Great Britain, under the title THE SILVER SWORD. This edition is published by Scholastic Inc., by arrangement with Criterion Books, Inc.

12 11 10 9 8 7 6 5 4 3 2   9/8 0 1 2 3/9

Printed in the U.S.A.   01

CONTENTS

NOTE

The characters in this book are fictitious, but the story is based upon fact. Imaginary names have been given to a few of the places mentioned — they are the villages of Boding and Kolina, the River Falken, the town of Falkenburg, and the prison camp of Zakyna. All other place names are real and can be found on the map of Europe. The description of the Red Army on the march is based on eye-witness accounts in J. Stransky's *East Wind over Prague*.

I. S.

Jan

CHAPTER 1

THE ESCAPE

Tнis is the story of a Polish family, and of what happened to them during the Second World War and immediately afterward. Their home was in a suburb of Warsaw, where the father, Joseph Balicki, was headmaster of a primary school. He and his Swiss wife, Margrit, had three children. In early 1940, the year when the Nazis took Joseph away to prison, Ruth, the eldest, was nearly thirteen, Edek was eleven, and the fair-haired Bronia three.

Warsaw under the Nazis was a place of terror, and without their father to protect them the Balickis had a grim time of it. But worse was in store for them. They were to endure hardships and conditions which made them think and plan and act more like adults than children. Great responsibilities were to fall upon Ruth. Many other girls had to face difficulties

1

as great as hers. But if there were any who faced them with as much courage, unselfishness, and common sense as she did, I have not heard of them.

First I must tell of Joseph Balicki and what happened to him in the prison camp of Zakyna.

The prison camp which the Nazis sent him to was in the mountains of South Poland. A few wooden huts clung to the edge of the bleak hillside. Day and night the wind beat down upon them, for the pine trees were thin and gave little shelter. For five months of the year snow lay thick upon the ground. It smothered the huts. It gave a coating of white fur to the twelve-foot double fence of wire that surrounded the clearing. In stormy weather it blew into the bare huts through cracks in the walls. There was no comfort in Zakyna.

The camp was crowded with prisoners. Most of them were Poles, but there were some Czechs, Hungarians, and a few Russians too. Each hut held about a hundred and twenty prisoners, yet it was hardly big enough for more than forty. They passed the time loafing about, playing chess, sewing, reading, fighting for old newspapers or cigarette stumps, quarreling, shouting. At mealtimes they huddled round trestle

tables to eat their cabbage and potato soup. It was the same for every meal. You could blow yourself out with it and never be satisfied. For drinking, they had warm water with bread crumbs in it — the Nazi guards called it coffee. Twice a week they had a dab of butter, and there was a teaspoonful of jam on Saturdays. What use was this for keeping out the cold?

Few had the strength or the spirit to escape. Several prisoners had gotten away — a few even reached the plains. Those that were not caught and sent back died of exposure in the mountains.

But Joseph was determined to escape. During the first winter he was too ill and dispirited to try. He would sit around the hut, thinking of his family and staring at the few tattered photos of them that he had been allowed to keep. He would think of his school in Warsaw and wonder what was happening there now. When the Nazis came, they had not closed it. But they had taken away the Polish textbooks and made him teach in German. They had hung pictures of Hitler in all the classrooms. Once, during a scripture lesson, Joseph had turned the picture of Hitler's face to the wall. Someone had reported this to the Nazis. Then the Nazi Storm Troops had come for Joseph in the middle of the night and bundled him off to Zakyna. They had left Margrit and the three children behind. How he longed to see them again!

During the summer his health mended, but the number of guards was doubled. A group of six — he was one of them — tried to break away together, but the attempt failed. For this he had a month of solitary confinement.

The following winter he was ill again, but no less determined to escape. He decided to wait till early spring, when the snow was beginning to melt and the nights were not so bitter.

Very carefully he laid his plans.

It was no use thinking of cutting the wire fence. There was a trip line inside the double fence, and anyone who crossed it would be shot.

If he got as far as touching the fence, the alarm bell in the guardhouse would ring. There was only one way out: the way the guards went, through the gate and past the guardhouse. His idea was to disguise himself as one of them and follow them as they went off duty. But how was he to get hold of the uniform?

At the back of each block was a leaky and unheated hut known as "the cooler." It had three or four cells to which unruly prisoners were sent to "cool off." To be sent there you only had to be late for roll call or talk back to a guard. It was a popular place in summer because it was so quiet. But in winter you could freeze to death there. In spring, with a bit of luck, you might survive a night or two of frost.

One March day, during the morning hut inspection, he flicked a paper pellet at the guard. It stung him behind the ear and made him turn round. The next one made his nose smart. That was all there was time for. Within five minutes Joseph was in a cell in the cooler.

For two days he stamped up and down, to keep himself warm. He clapped his arms against his sides. He dared not lie down for more than a few moments at a time in case he dropped off to sleep and never woke again. Twice a day a guard brought him food. For the rest of the time he was alone.

On the evening of the third day the guard came as usual. When Joseph heard the soft thud of his footsteps in the snow, he crouched down on the floor at the back of his tiny cell. He had a smooth round stone and a catapult in his hands. He had made the catapult from pine twigs and the elastic sides of his boots. His eyes were fixed on the flap in the door. In a moment the guard would unlock it, peer inside, and hand in the food.

Tensely, Joseph waited. He heard the key grate in the rusty lock of the outside door of the cooler. The hinges creaked open. There was the sound of a match spluttering — the guard was lighting the lamp. Heavy boots clumped across the floor toward his cell.

Joseph drew back the elastic. He heard the padlock on the flap being unlocked. The flap slid aside.

The guard had not seen Joseph when the stone struck him in the middle of the forehead and knocked him down. The floor shook as he tumbled. He groaned and rolled over.

Joseph must act quickly, before the guard came to his senses. He knew the guard kept his bunch of keys in his greatcoat pocket. He must get hold of them without delay. He must lift the guard till they were within reach.

He took a hook and line from under his bed. He had made the line by cutting thin strips from his blanket and plaiting them together. The hook was a bent four-inch nail that he had smuggled in from his hut.

After several attempts, the hook caught in the top button of the guard's greatcoat. Joseph tugged at the line and drew the guard, still groaning, up toward him . . . higher and higher.

Suddenly the line snapped. The guard fell back, striking his head sharply on the floor. The hook was lost.

Joseph had one spare hook — that was all.

He tried again. This time the button thread broke and the button went spinning across the floor.

He tried for the next button. Again the thread broke.

He had begun to despair when he saw the keys. They were lying on the floor. They had been shaken out of the greatcoat pocket when the guard fell.

Quickly Joseph fished for the ring of keys and hauled it up. A few moments later he was kneeling beside the senseless body, hastily stripping off the uniform. There was no time to lose.

Already the locking up of the prisoners had started and he could hear the guards shouting at them outside.

Joseph felt warm in the guard's uniform. The greatcoat reached to his ankles. The fur cap had flaps for covering his ears. He smiled to himself as he locked the guard in the freezing cell. Then, turning up his collar so that the tips touched his cheekbones, he went out into the bitter night.

He walked through the snow toward Block E, where the Hungarian and Rumanian prisoners were kept. In the dark shadows behind the huts he hid until the trumpet sounded the change of guard.

Hundreds of times he had watched the soldiers of the guard fall in and march out of camp. He had memorized every order, every movement. It seemed to him quite natural now to be lining up with the others.

"Anything to report?" the officer asked each of them in turn.

"All correct, sir," they answered.

"All correct, sir," said Joseph in his best German.

"Guard, dismiss!" said the officer.

Joseph dropped to the rear and followed the other soldiers out — out of the great spiked gate and into freedom. It seemed too good to be true.

Some of the soldiers stopped outside the guardhouse to gossip. A few went in. Joseph walked straight ahead, turning his head away from the window light as he passed.

"Where are you going?" one of them called.

"Shangri La," he muttered. It was the soldiers' name for the night club in the village, where they sometimes spent their off-duty times.

Without looking behind him, he walked on.

CHAPTER 2

JOURNEY THROUGH
THE AIR

THE village of Zakyna was a mile below the camp. It was a mass of tiny huts clinging to the steep cliffside. There was no moon that night, but Joseph could see lights in the windows.

He walked straight through the village.

Suddenly he was challenged in German. "Karl, give me the cigarettes," said a rough voice.

He took no notice and walked on.

"Karl, the cigarettes!" the voice shouted, threateningly.

He hurried on.

There were footsteps behind him.

He turned round to look. A drunken soldier was tottering after him.

Joseph began to run. The soldier ran too, swearing whenever he stumbled.

10

Just below the last huts in the village, the road curled away from the cliff edge. A mail car had pulled up. Its lights were on and the engine running. There was a pile of luggage in the road, and an angry group of people had gathered round.

"You're two hours late!" someone cried.

"I told you there was an avalanche. The road was blocked," returned the driver.

Joseph dived behind the white wall of snow that the snow plough had thrown up at the side of the road. He was right on the edge of the cliff, which dropped steeply into the darkness. He heard the sound of crates being dumped in the road. And he heard the drunken soldier roll up and cry, "Driver, you've pinched my cigarettes!"

"Chuck him over the cliff," said someone.

A scuffle. Laughter. Steps coming toward him.

Joseph slid quietly away to where a square shape jutted out from the road. In the dark it looked like a cart without wheels. Quickly he hid underneath.

At once he wished he hadn't moved. A heavy crate banged down on to the boards above his head. The boards quivered and shook. Boots scraped the wood, shuffled on the snow.

There was a babble of voices — jokes and leg pulling mixed with directions for the loading of the crates.

Joseph waited tensely while the crates were lifted in and the tarpaulin draped over them. When the soldiers were back in the road, he heaved himself over the wooden edge and under the tarpaulin.

A loud voice shouted, "Are you ready, there?"

From the other side of the dark valley came an answering call.

Suddenly Joseph realized that the wooden boards he lay on were moving. They were sliding out into the darkness, away from the road. Where was he?

As soon as he dared, he lifted the edge of the tarpaulin and looked out. He was in a kind of roofless cage. It was hung by pulleys and wire to an overhead cable and was swinging giddily from side to side. An aerial luggage lift. These were quite common in the mountains. They were driven by electricity and used for carrying goods from one side of a steep valley to the other.

Joseph sighed with relief. The giddy movement of the cage made him feel sick, but he knew that every second it was taking him farther from his enemies.

Then suddenly the cage squeaked to a standstill. It began to slide back, back to the road. The voices on the road grew louder. A jerk, a rattle of pulleys, the scrape of wood on snow, and he was back where he had started. Someone leapt into the cage and lifted the tarpaulin on the other side of the crates from Joseph.

"There's room for it alongside — hurry up!" cried the same voice.

Joseph's hand was in his revolver holster. He meant to fight his way out if he had to. But all he could feel in the holster was a stick of chocolate.

Another crate was chucked in and kicked alongside the other pair. It banged against his foot and nearly made him scream with pain. He fell back and bit his lip, groaning.

But no one heard his groans, for the cage was already rattling out into the darkness again. While he rubbed his bruised toes, it pitched and swung from side to side. After a few minutes of climbing, a shape loomed down toward him and rattled past. It was the balance lift — the descending cage which balanced the weight of the climbing one — and it meant he had passed the halfway mark. Ahead of him was the black shape of the mountain. With every swing of the cage and every creak of the cable, it came nearer. Were there soldiers on that side, too? If so, what was he to do? He could not escape discovery, and he was quite unarmed.

In a flash he made up his mind.

He lifted the tarpaulin from his shoulders and sat with his back to the crates, facing the dark mountain.

CHAPTER 3

THE HIDING PLACE

THE cage banged to a standstill. A flashlight shone full in Joseph's face.

"I have you covered with my pistol," said Joseph steadily. "If you make a sound, I'll shoot."

A Polish voice swore.

"Be quiet. Do you want me to shoot?" said Joseph. "Hand me your flashlight."

He seized it from the trembling hands and flashed the beam on to a gray-bearded peasant face. Joseph's spirits rose. The man was Polish, a countryman of his.

Joseph spoke more gently. "Do as I tell you, and you'll come to no harm. Unload the cage."

Joseph questioned him while he was unloading. "Is the cage worked from this end? The control is in your hands? Good. We shan't be disturbed, then. Take me to where you live."

The crates were safely stacked and the shed

by the cage locked. The peasant had kept one crate for himself. It contained provisions and clothing from town. He lifted it onto his shoulder and then led the way along a track of beaten snow that wound upward through pine trees. Soon they came to his home. It was a large chalet, with wide overhanging eaves. Wood was stacked at the sides.

He laid down the crate and led Joseph inside.

A wood fire was burning brightly in a wide, open hearth. A large pot hung above it from a hook in the chimney. An old lady was sitting by the fire. She looked startled.

Joseph threw his cap and greatcoat over a chair.

"Here's the pistol I almost shot you with," he said. "It's a slab of chocolate."

He broke it into three pieces, giving one to each of them. They were suspicious and waited till Joseph had swallowed his piece before they ate theirs.

"I don't understand," said the peasant slowly. "You speak like a Pole. You look like a Pole. But your uniform —"

At that moment a bell clanged out from the other side of the valley. It echoed among the mountains.

"That's the prison bell," said Joseph. "It's a

long time since it rang like that — when the last prisoner escaped."

"You've come to search for him?" asked the old lady.

"I am the prisoner," said Joseph. "I knocked out a guard and stole his uniform. Look if you don't believe me — here's my camp number burnt into my arm: ZAK 2473. I want you to hide me."

The number convinced them that he was telling the truth. They knew that if they were found hiding him they would die. But they were brave people and did not hesitate.

Joseph slept in a warm bed that night for the first time in two years.

In the morning the old man went to work the luggage lift as usual. Before going, he arranged a danger signal: if there were any soldiers coming across in the cage, he would whistle three times. And he showed Joseph a hiding place in the woodshed.

While he was away, Joseph showed the old woman the tattered photos of his family. He had taken them out of his wallet so many times to look at them that they were creased and crumpled and finger-marked all over. He spoke about his wife and children, his school, his capture by the Nazis; about the shortage of food, the destruction everywhere, and the continual fear of arrest. Every day had brought news of more families being split up.

The old woman was moved by his story. While he was speaking, she began to think of ways in which she could help him. He looked starved and needed good food. She had a little cheese and oatcakes, a side of bacon hanging in the cellar, and the remains of a tin of real coffee saved from before the war.

Suddenly there was a loud bang on the door. Was it a search party? If so, why had the old man given no warning?

A voice called out in German.

There was no time to escape to the woodshed.

"Quick — up there!" The old woman pointed up the chimney. "There's an opening on the right, halfway up."

Joseph dived into the hearth and hauled himself up over the iron spit. The fire was only smouldering, and there was not much smoke. He had not found the opening when the door burst open and two soldiers came in. While they searched the room, he stood very still, his legs astride the chimney. He wanted to cough. He thought his lungs would burst.

Suddenly a head peered up the chimney. It

was the old woman. "They've gone upstairs," she said. "But don't come down yet."

She showed him where the opening was. He crept inside, coughing. He could see the sky through the wide chimney top above him.

He was congratulating himself on his good luck when he heard the soldiers return to the room below. With difficulty he controlled his cough.

"What about the chimney?" said a German voice. "Plenty of room to hide up there."

"Plenty of soot too," said the other soldier. "Your uniform's older than mine. What about your going up?"

"Not likely."

"Then we'll send a couple of bullets up for luck."

Two ear-splitting explosions — it seemed as if the whole chalet was falling down. Joseph clung to his perch. There was a great tumbling about his ears. He clung and clung and clung — till his fingers were torn from their grip, and he fell.

When he came to his senses, he was lying on the floor. The old woman was bending over him, washing his face with cold water.

"It's all right — they've gone," she said. "The

fall of soot saved you. The soldiers ran for it
when the soot came down. They were afraid for
their uniforms."

"I'm sorry I didn't have time to warn you,"
said the old man. "The soldiers had hidden
themselves in the cage. I didn't see them till it
was too late."

Joseph spent two whole weeks in the chalet.
The old couple treated him like a son, sharing
all they had with him. They fed him so well that
his thin cheeks filled out and he gained several
pounds in weight. They were simple, homey
folk, and in their company his mind grew more
peaceful than it had been for years. In the
brutality of his prison life he had almost forgotten what kindness was.

He passed his time indoors, mostly eating and
resting. More than once he was tempted to go
outside. The spring sun beamed down all day
long from clear skies. It melted the icicles that
hung from the roof; it roused the first crocuses
from the bare brown patches in the snow. But
there was no sense in exposing himself, and he
wisely stayed indoors. The nights were freezing,
and he was glad of his warm blankets.

On the fifteenth night he left the chalet on
the first stage of the long journey home. The

moon was in its first quarter, and it was freezing hard. He was wearing the warm woolen clothes of a Polish highlander. The old man went with him as guide for three days, till they were clear of the high mountains.

On the afternoon of the second day they reached the edge of the snow line. Little rivers coursed down from under the snow. Wherever they trod, the ground was soggy and their boots squelched. But it was a joy to leave the snow behind and to see the snowdrops and crocuses everywhere. Lower down in the valleys the grass was already green, gay with primroses, violets, and wild daffodils.

In the gorge where the River Sanajec tumbles down between steep wooden rocks to meet the great rivers of the plains, they said good-by to each other. The old man took Joseph's head between his hands, blessed him, and wished him good fortune.

CHAPTER 4

THE SILVER SWORD

IT took Joseph four and a half weeks to walk to Warsaw. He had lived in the city all his life and knew it well. But now, on his return, there was hardly a street he recognized and not an undamaged building anywhere. The place was as bleak and silent as the craters of the moon. Instead of proud homes, he found crumbling walls; instead of streets, tracks of rubble between mountains of bricks. Windows were charred and glassless. Public buildings were burned-out shells.

In this wilderness people still managed to go on living. Joseph saw them wandering, pale and hungry-eyed, and vanish down paths of their own into the ruins. They had made their homes in cellars or had dug caves in the rubble. A few had even tried to make them look gay. A bomb gash in a cellar wall was draped with bright curtains. In another hole there was a window-box full of purple crocuses. Here and there a tree that had escaped blast damage sprouted with spring leaves.

But the only really lively place was the railway. The Nazis had to keep this clear, whatever the cost. Never had Joseph seen railway lines gleam as these did — eight lines of polished steel along which, day and night, the busy trains poured. Eastward with carriages of troops and trucks of ammunition, they carried war to Russia. Westward they brought back the wounded to Germany, and sometimes rich plunder from the Ukraine.

Joseph spent three days finding the street where he used to live. The school and school-house — his home — had disappeared.

There was a house opposite with a sign marked Polish Welfare. He made some inquiries there, but the people were new and could not help him. At another house he had better luck. He knew the woman who lived there — A Mrs. Krause, who had had a child at his school some years ago. In a small back room he questioned her eagerly about his family.

"The Nazis destroyed your school," she said.

"What happened to my wife?"

"They came for her in January last year,

during the night. It was just after Dr. Frank called for a million foreign workers to go to Germany. She's in Germany, probably working on the land. I'm a member of the Polish Council for Protection and we tried to trace her, but without success."

"And the children — did they go with her?" asked Joseph.

Mrs. Krause turned away. "I don't know anything about them," she said.

Joseph felt that she was hiding unpleasant news. He begged her to speak.

"I know nothing," she said.

"That's not true," he said. "As a member of the Council, you must have found out something."

At last, with a weary sigh, she told him all she knew. "On the night your wife was taken away, someone fired at the van from the attic of your house. A tire was punctured, and one of the Nazi soldiers was hit in the arm. But they got away with the van all the same. An hour later they sent a truckload of soldiers with explosives. They blew the whole place up. The children have not been seen since."

Joseph was too dazed to grasp all this at once, and Mrs. Krause had to repeat it. She told him of the efforts made to trace them, but it was obvious that she believed them to be dead.

Without a word Joseph got up and went out into the street. For the rest of the day he wandered among the ruins, too dazed to think. He spent the night in the burned-out shell of a bus station. In spite of the rain which fell through the roof, he slept.

He spent the next few days searching among the ruins for his children, with a kind of hopeless despair. At night he returned to the home of the Krauses, who fed him and gave him a bed.

One night Mrs. Krause said to him, "It's no use your going on like this. Your children are not alive. The house was locked before the soldiers left, and they must have died in the explosion. If you want to go on searching, search for your wife."

"Germany's a large place," said Joseph. "What hope should I have of finding her?"

"She might escape, as you did," said Mrs. Krause. "You must have known that something like this might happen. Did you never make any plans? Did you never fix a meeting place?"

Joseph thought for a moment. "Yes, as a matter of fact we did. We arranged that, if we were separated, we would try to make for Switzerland. My wife is Swiss, and her parents live there still."

Mrs. Krause took his hands in hers and smiled. "There's your answer, then. Go to Switzerland, and with God's help you will find her there."

"But the children — they may still be here," said Joseph.

He spent several more days looking for them.

One afternoon, while he was poking among the rubble of his old home, he found a tiny silver sword. About five inches long, it had a brass hilt engraved with a dragon breathing fire. It was a paper knife that he had once given to his wife for a birthday present.

While he was cleaning the blade on his jersey, he noticed that he was not alone. A small ragged boy sat watching him keenly. He had fair wispy hair and unnaturally bright eyes. Under one arm he had a wooden box, under the other a bony gray kitten.

For a moment Joseph thought it was his son, Edek. Then he realized that he was too small for Edek.

He walked over and stroked the kitten.

"What's his name?" he asked.

"He hasn't got a name. He's just mine," said the boy.

"What's *your* name?" said Joseph.

The boy pouted and hugged the wooden box under his arm. His eyes were shrewdly summing Joseph up. After a while, "Give me that sword," he said.

"But it's mine," said Joseph.

"You found it on my pitch. This is my place."

Joseph explained about his house and how this rubble was all that was left of it.

"I'll give you food for it," said the boy, and he offered Joseph a cheese sandwich.

"I have plenty," said Joseph. He put his hand into his pocket, but it was empty. He looked again at the boy's sandwich and saw it was one that Mrs. Krause had given him that morning, only rather grubby now.

"You little pickpocket!" he laughed. But before he could grab it back, the boy had swallowed most of it himself and given the rest to the cat, which was now purring contentedly.

After a while Joseph said, "I'm looking for my family. Ruth is the eldest — she'd be fifteen now, and tall and fair. Then Edek, he'd be thirteen. Bronia is the youngest — she'd be five." He described them briefly, told him what he knew of their fate and asked if the boy had seen them.

The boy shrugged his shoulders. "Warsaw is full of lost children," he said. "They're dirty and starving, and they all look alike."

His words made him sound indifferent. But Joseph noticed that the boy had listened carefully and seemed to be storing up everything in the back of his mind.

"I'll give you this sword on one condition," said Joseph. "I'm not sure that my children *are* dead. If ever you see Ruth or Edek or Bronia, you must tell them about our meeting. Tell them I'm going to Switzerland to find their mother.

To their grandparents' home. Tell them to follow as soon as they can."

The boy grabbed the sword before Joseph had time to change his mind. He popped it into the little wooden box, picked up the cat, and ran off.

"I'll tell you more about them tomorrow," Joseph called after him. "Meet you here in the morning — and don't let me down."

The boy vanished.

CHAPTER 5

THE GOODS TRAIN

J OSEPH did not expect the boy to keep his appointment with him in the morning. But he was there, sitting on the rubble with his cat and his wooden box, waiting for him.

"It's no use your trying to pick my pockets this morning," said Joseph, sitting down beside him.

"You've pinned the flaps," said the boy. "But that doesn't make any difference."

Joseph moved away a couple of paces. "Keep your hands off," he said. "Now, listen. I'm starting off for Switzerland tonight. I don't want to walk all the way, so I'm going to jump a train. Where's the best place?"

"You will be caught and shot," said the boy. "Or you will freeze to death in the trucks. The nights are bitter. Your hair will be white with frost; your fingers will turn to icicles. And when

30

the Nazis find you, you will be stiff as the boards at the bottom of the truck. That is what happens to those who jump trains."

"You seem to know a lot about it," said Joseph.

"I have seen it," said the boy.

"Can't be helped. I must risk it," said Joseph. "Better than going back to the place I've come from."

"I'll take you to the bend where the trains slow down," said the boy. He jumped up and began running.

Joseph had a job to keep up with him. But the boy could run and talk and point out the landmarks and stuff food into his mouth and the cat's, all at the same time.

Joseph tried to find out something about this extraordinary boy. What was his name? Where did he live? Were his parents still alive? But the boy would tell him nothing.

They came to the railway and followed the track past the station to a large bend. Here, beside a train shed, they sat down to watch.

"All the trains slow down here," said the boy. "You will find no better place to jump on."

They saw several trains pass westward. One of them was a goods train, and it went more slowly than the rest. Would there be a goods

train passing that way tonight? Joseph thought
he could jump it without danger.

"Let's have something to eat," said Joseph,
and he unpinned the flaps of his pockets. But
his hands went straight through and came out
into the daylight. He looked at the boy watching
the trains, still chewing. He looked at the cat,
curled and purring in the boy's lap. He knew
where his sandwiches were now.

"You little devil!" he cried. "Just wait till I
catch you."

But the boy had vanished.

He didn't see him again till after dark, after
he had said goodbye to the Krauses and left their
house for the last time. The boy was waiting for
him at the bottom of the street.

"Ssh!" said the boy. "We must go by the back
way — it's curfew time. If the Nazi patrols see
us, they'll shoot."

"What's all that you're carrying?" said Joseph.

He looked closer and saw that the boy's
ragged shirt was stuffed with long loaves, like
monster cigars.

"Mother in heaven! Where did you get all
that lot from?"

"I borrowed them," said the boy. "I know the
canteen at the Nazi barracks. There's plenty in
the bakehouse there. Take them — you'll be
hungry."

"Ought to see me through to America, that lot," said Joseph, as he took them. "What about yourself? You've some appetite, if I remember rightly."

"I borrow for everybody," said the boy. "They always send me. I'm so small I can wriggle under the barbed wire. I run so fast the soldiers can never catch me. And if — " He broke off suddenly. "Lie down. Patrol coming."

They dropped behind a wall and lay flat till the patrol had passed. Then they hurried by the back way to the railway. They almost ran into another patrol, and there were shots in the darkness. But the boy knew the ruins better than the patrol, and they got away.

They came to the bend where Joseph intended to jump, and they hid beside an empty warehouse. It was drizzling. The warehouse was littered with broken glass and charred timber. It was open to the sky except at one corner, where a strip of iron roof curled over. Under this they sheltered from the wet. A train clattered by, with a churning of pistons and a great hiss of steam. The long carriages clanked into the darkness, and the red light on the guard's van faded.

"Too fast for me," thought Joseph. "I must wait for a goods train."

As they sat there waiting, Joseph said, "I have

much to thank you for, and I don't even know your name."

The boy said nothing, but went on stroking the cat.

The drizzle turned to heavy rain. The drops danced on the roof, which creaked at every gust of wind.

"Have you no parents?" said Joseph.

"I have my gray cat and this box," he said.

"You won't come with me?" said Joseph.

The boy ignored the question. He was undoing the wooden box, and he took out the little silver sword. "This is the best of my treasures," he said. "It will bring me luck. And it will bring you luck, because you gave it to me. I don't tell anybody my name — it is not safe. But because you gave me the sword and I didn't borrow it, I will tell you." He whispered. "It is Jan."

"There are many Jan's in Poland, what's your surname?"

"That's all. Just Jan."

Joseph did not question him further. "Stay here in the dry," he said when it was time to go. But Jan insisted on going with him.

They crouched down beside the main track.

A train came along — was it a goods train? By the light of a signal lamp they saw red crosses painted on the carriages, streaming with rain.

A hospital train. The blinds were down. Except for an occasional blur where one had worn thin, no light peeped through.

At last, when Joseph had almost given up hope, a goods train came. The first few trucks rumbled slowly past.

"Good-by, Jan. Remember your promise Whatever happens, I shall not forget you. God bless you."

Joseph chose an empty truck and ran alongside at the same speed as the train. Darkness swallowed him. Jan did not see him jump.

One by one the heavy, dismal, sodden trucks clanked by. Last of all, the small red light, so dim that it hardly showed. Then the shrill note of a whistle, as the train gathered speed beyond the bend.

It was raining heavily now.

Jan was soon soaked to the skin. He hurried away through the dark streets. He had tucked the gray cat inside his jacket. It was almost as wet as he was and hardly warm at all. Under his arm he hugged the wooden box. And he thought of the silver sword inside.

CHAPTER 6

THE NIGHT
OF THE
STORM TROOPERS

WHAT had happened to Joseph's family that night, over a year ago, when the Nazi storm troopers called at the schoolhouse? Was what Mrs. Krause said true? Had they taken his wife away? Had they returned and blown up the house with the children in it?

This is what happened:

That night there was an inch of snow on the roofs of Warsaw. Ruth and Bronia were asleep in the bedroom next to their mother's. Edek's room was on the top floor, below the attic. He was asleep when the Nazi soldiers broke into the house, but he woke up when he heard a noise outside his door. He jumped out of bed and turned the handle. The door was locked. He shouted and banged on it with his fists, but it was no use. Then he lay down with his ear to the floor and listened. In his mother's room the men were rapping out orders, but he could not catch a word that was said.

In the ceiling was a small trapdoor that led into the attic. A ladder lay between his bed and the wall. Quietly he removed it, hooked it under the trap, and climbed up.

Hidden between the water tank and the felt jacket round it was his rifle. He was a member of the Boys' Rifle Brigade and had used it in the siege of Warsaw. It was loaded. He took it out and quickly climbed down to his room.

The noise in the room below had stopped. Looking out of the window into the street, he saw a Nazi van waiting outside the front door. Two Storm Troopers were taking his mother down the steps, and she was struggling.

Quietly Edek lifted the window sash till it was half open. He dared not shoot in case he hit his mother. He had to wait till she was in the van and the doors were being closed.

His first shot hit a soldier in the arm. Yelling, the soldier jumped in beside the driver. The next two shots Edek aimed at the tires. One punctured the rear wheel, but the van got away, skidding and roaring up the street. His other shots went wide.

With the butt of his rifle he broke down the door and ran down to his sisters. They were locked in, too. He burst open the door.

Bronia was sitting up in bed and Ruth was trying to calm her. She was almost as distraught herself. Only the effort to comfort Bronia kept her from losing control.

"I hit one of the swine," said Edek.

"That was very silly of you," said Ruth. "They'll come back for us now."

"I couldn't let them take Mother away like that," said Edek. "Oh, be quiet, Bronia! Howling won't help."

"We must get away from here before they come back," said Ruth.

With some difficulty she dressed Bronia, while Edek went into the hall to fetch overcoats and boots and fur caps.

There was no time for Ruth to dress properly. She put on a coat over her nightdress and wound a woolen scarf round Bronia.

"We can't get out the front way," said Edek. "There's another van coming. I heard the whistle."

"What about the back?" said Ruth.

"The wall's too high. We'd never get Bronia

over. Besides, there are Nazis billeted in that street. There's only one way: over the roof."

"We'll never manage that," said Ruth.

"It's the only way," said Edek. "I'll carry Bronia. Be quick — I can hear them coming."

He picked up the sobbing Bronia and led the way upstairs. He was wearing his father's thick overcoat over his pajamas, a pair of stout boots on his bare feet, and his rifle slung on his back.

When they were all up in the attic, he smashed the skylight.

"Now listen, Bronia," said Edek. "If you make a sound, we shall never see Mother again. We shall all be killed."

"Of course we shall see her again," Ruth added. "But only if you do as Edek says."

He climbed through the skylight on to the slippery roof. Ruth handed Bronia up to him, then followed herself. The bitterly cold air made her gasp.

"I can't carry you yet, Bronia," said Edek. "You must walk behind me and hold on to the rifle. It doesn't matter if you slip, if you hold on to the rifle. And don't look down."

The first few steps — as far as the V between the chimney and the roof ridge — were ghastly. Edek made a dash for it, grabbed the telephone bracket and hauled himself up, with Bronia clinging on behind. She was speechless with terror. He reached back and hauled Ruth up after him.

After a few moments' rest, they slid down a few feet on to a flat part that jutted out, a sort of parapet.

The roof ridge lay between them and the street, so they could not see what was happening down there. But they could hear shouting, the whine of cars, the screech of brakes.

Luckily for them, all the houses on this side of the school were joined together in one long terrace; otherwise they could not have got away. Even so, it was a miracle that none of their slips and tumbles ended in disaster.

They must have gone fully a hundred yards when the first explosion shook the air. A sheet of fire leapt up from their home into the frosty night sky. They fell flat in the snow and lay there. The roof shook; the whole city seemed to tremble. Another explosion. Smoke and flames poured from the windows. Sparks showered into the darkness.

"Come along," said Edek. "We shan't let them have us now."

With growing confidence, they hurried along the roof-tops. At last, by descending a twisted fire escape, they reached street level. On and on they hurried, not knowing or caring where they went as long as they left those roaring flames behind them. They did not stop till the fire was far away and the pale winter dawn was breaking.

They took shelter in the cellar of a bombed house. Exhausted, huddled together for warmth, they slept till long after midday, when cold and hunger woke them.

CHAPTER 7

WINTER AND SUMMER HOMES

THEY made their new home in a cellar at the other end of the city. They had tunneled their way into it. From the street it looked like a rabbit's burrow in a mound of rubble, with part of a wall rising behind. On the far side there was a hole in the lower part of the wall, and this let in light and air as well as rain.

When they asked the Polish Council of Protection about their mother, they were told she had been taken off to Germany to work on the land. Nobody could say which part of Germany. Though they went many times to ask, they never found out any more. "The war will end soon," they were told. "Be patient, and your mother will come back." But the war dragged on, and their patience was to be sorely tried.

They quickly made their new home as comfortable as they could. Edek, who could climb like a monkey, scaled three stories of a bombed building to fetch a mattress and some curtains. The mattress he gave to Ruth and Bronia. The curtains made good sheets. On wet days they could be used over the hole in the wall to keep the rain out. With floorboards he made two beds, chairs, and a table. With bricks from the rubble he built a wall to divide the cellar into two rooms, one to live in and one to sleep in. He stole blankets from a Nazi supply dump, one for each of them. Here they lived for the rest of that winter and the following spring.

Food was not easy to find. Ruth and Bronia had green Polish ration cards and were allowed to draw the small rations that the Nazis allowed. But, except when Edek found casual work, they had no money to buy food. Edek had no ration card. He had not dared to apply for one, as that would have meant disclosing his age. Everyone over twelve had to register, and he would almost certainly have been carried off to Germany as a slave worker. Whenever possible, they ate at the soup kitchens which Polish Welfare had set up. Sometimes they begged at a nearby convent. Sometimes they stole from the Nazis or scrounged from their garbage bins. They saw nothing wrong in stealing from their enemies, but they were careful never to steal from their own people.

War had made Edek sharp and self-reliant for his years. Ruth was slower to adapt herself to the new life. At first, during that long-drawn-out winter and the biting winds of early spring, it seemed as if she were too young to take on responsibility. But she learned gradually. She saw that Edek was always cheerful — because he was always busy. She knew she must get out of the habit of leaving all the practical details to him. One thing she could do was to make Bronia less miserable. She remembered that Bronia had always loved drawing. Ever since her little fist had been able to hold a pencil, she had delighted her father with her scribbling. So Ruth encouraged her to go on drawing now. They had no pencils or paper, but they had the cellar walls and plenty of charred wood from which to make charcoal. Bronia drew what she saw. Soon the walls were covered with pictures of people queueing outside the soup kitchen and of children playing hide-and-seek among the ruins.

Then Ruth started a school. She invited other lost children of Bronia's age and a little older. While Edek was out at work or finding food, she

told them stories in the cellar. When she ran
out of stories, the others took their turn. She
made them speak out clearly, without mum-
bling. One day at the soup kitchen she talked
about her school. Next time she went she was
given slates and chalk and a pocket Bible. News
of these presents spread like a heath fire, and
soon she had a mob of urchins outside the cellar
window, begging to be allowed to join the
school. But there was only room for twelve, and
very reluctantly she had to turn them away.

Ruth was a born teacher. She could hold the
children spellbound for as long as she liked. She
varied the work as much as possible, giving the
mornings to lessons and the afternoons to play.
The day started with a Bible story. She read it
herself, with the children round her — three to
a blanket if it was cold. Next came reading and
writing, followed by a break in the open air. Up
they shot from their rabbits' warren into the
sunlight. They ran down the street to the
wooden fence which they called "the Riviera."
Here they would sit in a long line, pressing their
backs to the sun-drenched wood, soaking up the
warmth till their bodies were glowing all over.
On sunless days they played a brisk game before
returning to the cellar for another story.

They liked the stories from the Old Testament

best. Their favorite was always Daniel in the lions' den. They enjoyed it just as a story, but for Ruth it had a deeper meaning. She thought of it as the story of their own troubles. The lions were the cold and the hunger and the hardships of their life. If only they were patient and trustful like Daniel, they would be delivered from them. She remembered a picture of Daniel that her mother had once given her. He was standing in the dungeon, with his hands chained behind him and his face lifted toward a small barred window high above his head. He was smiling, and did not notice the lions that prowled about his feet, powerless to touch him. At night she liked to fall asleep with this picture in her mind. She could not always see it clearly. Sometimes Daniel's face was clouded and the light from the window fell upon the lions. They were scowling and snarling, and they filled her dreams with terror.

In the early summer the children left the city and went to live in the woods outside. It was cold at night out in the open. They slept huddled together in their blankets under an oak tree which Edek had chosen for the shelter of its branches. There was not much rain that summer, though they had one or two drenchings in May. After that Edek cut down some branches, lashed

them together, and made a lean-to. This was
thick enough to keep out all but the heaviest
rain.

Life was much healthier here than in the city.
The sun browned their limbs. There were plenty
of other families to play with, some of them
Jews who had escaped from the Warsaw ghetto.
They could run about freely and hold their
classes under the trees, without having to keep
a lookout for police patrols. Sometimes Ruth had
as many as twenty-five in her school. She would
have taken more, but they had no paper, very
few slates, and no books at all. Occasionally they
received a smuggled copy of a secret journal
specially published for children by the Polish
Underground press. It was called *Biedronka*,
"The Ladybird," and was full of the kind of
stories and pictures and jokes that children
enjoy. The grubby finger marks showed that
other families had seen it before them. When
Ruth's children had finished with it, there was
nothing left but a few tattered strips.

Because of the kindness of the peasants, food
was more plentiful. Though they were forbidden
to store food or to sell it to anyone but the Nazis,
they gave the children whatever they could
spare. They hid it, too, in cellars, in haystacks,
in holes in the ground. With the help of the

older children they smuggled it to the towns and sold it to the Poles on the black market.

Edek was one of the chief smugglers. In return for his services, he was given all the food he needed for the family. One of his dodges was to go off to town with pats of butter sewn into the lining of his coat. But he could only do this on cool days or at night. On hot days the butter melted. So he preferred to work at night if he could. In time the Germans became wary and posted patrols on all the main roads into the city. After that he cut across country, using paths and rough tracks. He was well aware of the penalties if he were caught. A younger child might get away with a beating, but boys as strong as he was would be carried off to Germany, for the Nazis were getting short of labor at home.

Another of Edek's dodges was the cartload of logs which he drove into the suburbs. Some of the logs were split, their centers scraped out and packed with butter and eggs, then glued together again. Once he drove his cartload into a police patrol, which was searching everything on the road. They emptied the logs on to the pavement. Edek didn't stay to see if the glue would stand up to that treatment. He dived into the crowd and made off. Police

whistles were blowing and the chase had started, when some kind friend lifted him up and pitched him head first into a garbage cart. Here he lay hidden, under cinders and dust and rotting vegetables. After that, Edek did all his smuggling at night.

There came a morning, toward the end of August, when he failed to return. Ruth questioned other families in the forest, but no one had seen him. After some days of searching, she traced him to a village ten miles away. Edek had called at a house there while the secret police were searching for hidden stores. They had found cheese sewn into the lining of his coat. After setting fire to the house, they had taken him away in the van, with the house owner as well.

Ruth returned to the forest with a heavy heart, dreading to break the news to Bronia. Edek had been their lifeline. Food, clothes, money — they depended on him for all of these. In the city he had made a home out of a ruin. In the woods no tree gave better shelter than the oak he had chosen. And after dark, when the wind blew cold and the damp oozed out of the ground, none knew better than he how to keep the fire in untended till dawn, so that the glow from the embers should warm them all night as they slept.

Now Ruth and Bronia must fend for themselves. It was an ordeal before which the bravest spirit might quail.

CHAPTER 8

THE NEWCOMER

Two years passed without any news of Edek. Ruth and Bronia returned to Warsaw each winter and back to the woods again the following summer.

It was the summer of 1944. Out in the woods they began to realize that things were changing. Day and night the air was full of planes. From the distant city they could hear the boom of guns and the explosion of bombs. It was rumoured that the Nazis were on the defensive. Though the children did not know it till later, the Russian Marshal Rokossovsky was sweeping westward with seven great army groups, driving the Nazis before him. Moscow had broadcast a call to the resistance in Warsaw: "Poles, the hour of freedom is at hand! Poles, to arms! Do not lose a moment. The suburbs of Warsaw are already within range of Russian guns."

At once the Poles, under their own General Bor, rose up against the German garrison. At five o'clock, on the afternoon of August 1, a bomb went off in the Nazi Gestapo headquarters. At the same moment thousands of windows in the city were flung open, and a hail of bullets struck the passing Germans. All traffic ceased as the Polish underground rushed to the attack. Starving people streamed out of the cellars and flung themselves upon the Nazis, attacking with weapons if they had them, with their fists if they had nothing else.

But the Germans counterattacked from their strongholds. Hastily they concentrated five divisions, and their Tiger tanks drove a wedge through the city as far as the Vistula. The Soviet troops outside withdrew six miles under orders from Moscow, leaving the Poles to fight their own battle.

General Bor was short of arms and ammunition, and could not continue the struggle alone. He radioed for help to Britain and America. But the British and Americans were too busy fighting the Nazis in the west. Prime Minister Churchill cabled to Stalin a request to help the Poles, but Stalin refused. He even refused to allow British and American planes carrying supplies to land on Soviet airfields. So the Poles, desperately short of food and arms, were left to fight it out to the bitter end.

A few stragglers from the city, turned out by the Nazis to find their own safety, reached the woods. From them Ruth learned of Nazis having to fight for every inch of ground, of Poles tearing up the pavement slabs and using them as barricades in the streets, and of a message sent to the Pope by the women of Warsaw: "Most Holy Father, for three weeks we have lacked food and medicine. Warsaw is in ruins. No one is helping us. The world is ignorant of our fight."

On October 2, the sixty-third day of fighting, when the defenders had no more ammunition left, Warsaw broadcast its last appeal to the people of the world: "Without help, this struggle has become hopeless. God is righteous, and in His omnipotence He will punish all those responsible for this terrible injury to the Polish nation."

Too late to save the gallant defenders, Stalin changed his plans and ordered the Russians to march. By January 1945 the Nazis had gone and Warsaw was in Russian hands.

Because of the fighting, Ruth and Bronia had put off their return to the city till as late as possible. They had left it till winter had

already set in and cold and hunger drove them
and other families from the woods.

A rude shock awaited them. The Warsaw
they had known and lived in all their lives had
vanished. The Old Town had been wiped out,
and there were no streets left. Food was shorter
than it had ever been — only a little flour, fat
and sugar, no milk at all. Luckily, there was
water. Though the mains had been damaged,
fresh wells had been dug.

Somehow they found their way to the cellar
that had been their home for two years. There
were signs that it had been occupied during
the summer, then abandoned. The chairs and
beds had gone — probably used as firewood —
and the table was broken. There was a dark
hole at one end, which Ruth found to be the
beginning of a tunnel. It led under the street,
joining up with other cellars, other homes. Because of the firing and bombing, nobody had
used the streets unless he had to. With the help
of this clever network of tunnels, the brave
defenders had kept the struggle going all
autumn.

Patiently and without despair, Ruth set to
work to repair the damage. They had no beds,
but they still had the blankets they had brought
with them from the woods. Friends provided

them with sacks to sleep on. Some boys in Ruth's class mended the table and made chairs from boxes.

When all was as straight as she could make it, Ruth started up her school again. Some sixteen children were squeezed into the cellar; lessons were always undercover now. One day something happened which was to change the whole course of her life and to give hope to her flagging spirit.

It was a sunny day, and for once there was no firing. The children were out of doors playing a game called Air-raid Alert. One of them would cry "Alert!" and count to fifty while the others ran for shelter before he shouted "Stop!" Anyone who had not found a hiding place by then had to lie down and pretend to be dead.

Suddenly Bronia, who was very proud because she had never been dead yet, came running down to Ruth in the cellar.

"There's a boy lying down outside, and he won't get up," she cried.

"Tickle his ribs," said Ruth.

"I don't think he can get up," said Bronia.

"Who is it?"

"It's not one of the class. I've never seen him before."

Ruth went out to investigate. Lying on a heap of rubble was a ragged boy who might have been any age between nine and thirteen. His cheeks were thin and pale, and his eyes were closed. A mangy cock, with more bone than feather, stood by his head and squawked at anyone who went near him.

Ruth chased the cock away and knelt beside the boy. "Does anyone know who he is?" she asked the ring of children round her.

Nobody did.

"He looks ill and starved," said Ruth. "Yankel, will you help me lift him down to the cellar? And, Eva, please find something for him to eat — some soup if you can get it."

They carried him down to the cellar and laid him gently on the sacks. After a little while he opened his eyes.

"Where's Jimpy?" he said.

"We'll find Jimpy later," said Ruth. "I think you must have fainted. You'll be all right in a minute."

"I want Jimpy," said the boy.

"Perhaps Jimpy's the name of the cock," said Bronia.

"Yankel, go and fetch the cock," said Ruth.

"No fear! He's bitten me twice," said Yankel.

Ruth was going to fetch it herself, when the

cock appeared suddenly in the hole in the wall, squawked, flapped its dusty wings, and jumped down beside the boy.

"Jimpy, Jimpy!" said the boy, and he reached out his arms towards the mangy creature.

"He's a fine cock and he's got a fine name," said Ruth. "What's your name?"

"Shan't tell you," snapped the boy.

"Look, Eva's brought some soup for you," said Ruth. "You'll feel better in a minute. Sit up and drink it."

"He won't tell us his name," Bronia confided to the crowd at the door.

A girl pushed through the crowd and went over to Ruth. She had something in her hand.

"I found this in the street where he was lying," she said. "I think it must be his."

It was a small wooden box. Bronia seized it.

"It's heavy and it rattles. He must be rich," she cried. "Ruth, may we undo the string?"

"Give the box to him," said Ruth. "Nobody shall touch it without asking him."

The boy took the wooden box and smiled. Everyone wanted to look inside, but he wouldn't open it. However, he told them his name. It was Jan.

CHAPTER 9

THE RUSSIAN SENTRY

For some days Jan was too ill to leave. What he needed was rest, warmth, and good solid food. The children scrounged what food they could — it was easier to get now that the Russians had come — and left the nursing to Ruth. Jan had wrapped his wooden box in a piece of sacking which he used as a pillow, and lay on the floor quite contented. Jimpy the cock stood over him as bodyguard, and Ruth was the only person it would allow near him.

By the time Jan was better, he didn't want to go. So he made his home with Ruth and Bronia, and became one of the family. Bronia was very curious to know what was in the wooden box, but Jan never opened it. There was no chance for anyone else to open it either, for he carried it about with him wherever he went.

Several streets away there had appeared a brand-new hut, which was a Russian control post. One afternoon Ruth called there.

"Don't stand there staring at me, little girl," said the burly sentry who was on duty.

"I'm not a little girl. I'll be eighteen next week," said Ruth. "And I want to see your officer."

"The whole of Warsaw wants to see my officer. Run away and play."

"It's very important."

"Run away."

Ruth was angry. "It's all right for you. You've got plenty to eat and drink and warm clothes, too, and a bed to sleep in. Didn't you come here to set us free? You must let me see your officer."

The sentry grinned. "Well, seeing it's your birthday next week, I might stretch a point. But I don't hold out much hope that he'll see you."

He disappeared inside the post. A moment later he came out.

"The lieutenant says come back the year after next," said the sentry.

But before he realized what had happened, Ruth had pushed past him and into the post.

A worried-looking lieutenant was sitting at a desk, typing.

"Hey, you young hussy, come out!" cried the sentry.

"Leave her to me, Ivan," said the lieutenant, and Ivan went out, swearing under his breath.

"You're a determined young lady," said the lieutenant.

"I'm not a little girl, anyway," said Ruth.

"What is it you want?"

"I want food and clothes and blankets, pencils, and as much paper as you can spare. I've got sixteen children —"

The lieutenant gasped and nearly fell into the wastepaper basket.

"Seventeen, if you count the one that's lost. He really is mine — he's my brother, Edek. So is my sister, Bronia. The others are just my school. They're all half starving, and they're keen to learn and they've got nothing to write on. And I want you to help me to find Edek. He's been lost over a year."

"Anything else you'd like me to do?" said the lieutenant. He waved a thick pad of papers. "See this file? It's full of missing people, about ten to each page. All Warsaw's missing. Hopeless."

"One more name won't make a lot of difference," said Ruth.

"I might as well burn the lot for all the good it is."

"Oh, don't do that," said Ruth. "I see the writing's only on one side. Give me the papers, and we can use the blank sides in school for writing on."

The lieutenant laughed, and Ruth laughed too. "Sit down," he said, "and I'll take your particulars. But I warn you, nothing will come of it."

Before going, she was told to call back the next day. She called — and found a pound of sugar, a pound of flour, and six blankets waiting for her.

"It's more than you deserve, you little hussy," said Ivan. "Sign here. And your address."

She wrote "Bombed cellar" and told him where it was.

A week later, with the help of the sugar and flour, a wood fire, and a biscuit tin for an oven, she was preparing a birthday tea. Most of the children had been invited. Suddenly she heard sounds of a scuffle outside.

She ran out and saw a soldier being attacked by a boy. There was a flash of a knife near the soldier's neck, and Jimpy the cock was squawking and pecking at his ankles.

"Jan, drop that knife at once!" she cried. "Drop it — d'you hear me?"

She flung herself into the struggle. They all rolled over in a heap, but she had caught Jan by the wrist and knocked the knife out of his hand.

"That's a pretty welcome, I must say," said Ivan the sentry, as he picked up his cap and knocked the dust off. He tried to put it on his head, but the cock jumped on his shoulder and pecked his ear.

Ruth drove it away, then picked up the fallen knife.

"Don't you understand, Jan, they're our friends?" said Ruth.

"They're soldiers," said Jan sulkily.

"They're Russian soldiers, not Nazis. They've come to set us free and look after us."

"I hate soldiers. They're all the same," said Jan. "I hate them."

"I'm sorry about him, Ivan," said Ruth. "His manners are as bad as Jimpy's. Come inside. We're going to have a party. Come in, Jan."

Everyone went in except Jan, who stayed outside, sulking.

"So I chose the right day to call, little gir —
young lady," said Ivan. "My word, a birthday!
Too old to have them myself."

"You shall have the seat of honor, Ivan,"
said Ruth. And she gave him a box to sit on.

Ivan sat down — and got up rather quickly,
rubbing his seat.

"Two inches of rusty nail! That's not the sort
of honor I appreciate," he said. "Did nobody
ever teach you how to use a hammer?"

"I haven't got a hammer. I used half a brick,"
said Ruth. And picking up a piece of brick from

the floor, she flattened the offending nail so that Ivan could sit down without further injury.

"Brought a present for you," said Ivan, when he had settled comfortably. "Nothing much. But my kids at home are fond of it. Bar of chocolate."

"What's chocolate?" said Bronia, while Ruth thanked him.

She wasn't the only one who wanted to know what chocolate was. There were fifteen in the cellar. Ruth divided it into fifteen.

"Just about a crumb each. They won't tell from that. Wish I'd brought some more," said Ivan. "But I didn't come here to bring chocolate. I've got news for you, little gir — young lady. We've traced your brother Edek. He's in a transit camp at Posen."

Ruth threw her arms round his neck.

"What would the wife say if she could see me now?" said Ivan, and he planted a loud kiss on Ruth's cheek. Then he returned to the business in hand. "Of course, I had to handle the matter myself. If the lieutenant had done it, nothing would have come of it." He handed her a slip of paper, on which the name of the camp was written. "And here's something else might come in handy." He gave her a large packet of typewriting paper and a bundle of pencils.

Bronia clapped her hands for joy. "I'll draw lots of pictures of you, Ivan — rolling on the floor, and having your ear pecked, and sitting on the nail," she said, then added, "Did you pay for this all by yourself?"

"That's not the way we do things in the army," said Ivan.

"I hope you didn't steal it," said Ruth.

"And that's not the word we use for it," said Ivan. "Just tidied it up, you might say. It's a help to you and it's a help to the lieutenant, because he can't wear himself out typing any more."

"Don't tell Jan," said Ruth. "He's a dreadful thief, and it will only make him worse."

At that moment she saw Jan standing in the doorway. He was sobbing.

"Cheer up, son. I've forgiven you, even if you did want to cut off my head for a souvenir," said Ivan.

But there was something for which Jan had not forgiven him. He held out his little wooden box. It was in pieces. "You rolled on it, you great brute, and broke it," he said.

"I'll mend it for you," said Ivan.

Jan shook his head fiercely.

"Jan, can't you stop hating for one moment?" said Ruth.

As Jan clutched the broken pieces to his chest, something fell to the ground. It was the silver sword that Joseph had given him more than two years before.

Ruth picked it up and looked at it very closely. It was vaguely familiar — that dragon on the brass hilt — where had she seen it before? Then suddenly she recognized it as the birthday present her father had given her mother the last year before the war. Then she, too, began sobbing.

"Waterworks!" said Ivan, puzzled and embarrassed. "First it was 'kill me,' then it was 'kiss me,' and now it's the waterworks. Pardon me if I step outside and fetch my umbrella."

And he went back to his control post, wondering what to make of it all.

CHAPTER 10

MORE HELP
FROM IVAN

WHILE Bronia slept, Ruth and Jan sat up late that night, talking. There was much she wanted to know about her father, and Jan told her the little that he remembered. Why had the boy not spoken earlier about him? Surely he had been told the children's names? But Jan had forgotten them. War does strange things to young people. Months of strain had blotted from his memory many of the details of his meeting with Joseph. But he remembered two things: the determination on Joseph's face, and the name of the country he was bound for — Switzerland.

Long after Jan fell asleep, Ruth lay awake, thinking. Edek had been traced. Her father had escaped from prison and been seen alive and

free. How different must their future be now!
But it was confusing — so much had happened
so quickly.

By morning she had sorted things out and
knew what she must do. She explained the
situation to Bronia.

"We must leave Warsaw for good and go and
find Father," she said.

"Find Mother too?"

"Yes, Mother too. We must go to Switzerland."

"Where's that?"

"Millions of miles away," said Jan. "And you'll
have to walk, without any shoes."

"We'll have to walk some of the way," said
Ruth. "But Ivan will give us shoes, and we'll get
lifts on lorries and trains as well. It won't be so
bad now that spring's coming, and in summer
it will be lovely sleeping out under the stars.
We'll go to Posen first. It's not much out of our
way, and it's only two hundred miles. We can
beg for food, as we do now."

"I'll steal it," said Jan. "You leave that to me."

"I'm glad you want to come with us, Jan,"
said Ruth. "We need you to protect us."

"I've got my knife," said Jan.

"That will be very useful if you use it for
what it's meant for," said Ruth.

She went to see Ivan to explain matters and to ask him for shoes.

"I'll bring you anything I can," he said, "but tie up that cock next time I call."

He called the following week with shoes for each of them. They saw him coming, and Ruth told Jan to tie up Jimpy. He didn't like doing it, but he obeyed.

"Hello, you starving ragamuffins," said Ivan. "You've not grown much fatter. Why don't you put him in the pot?"

"Put who in the pot?" said Ruth.

Ivan jerked a thumb at Jimpy the cock, who was nearly strangling himself to break free of the string.

"He's my friend," said Jan indignantly. "I don't eat my friends."

Ivan grunted. "I admit he's a bit stringy. Not much gravy from him. If you put a flea through the mangle, you'd get more juice."

Jan's fingers ran to his knife.

Ivan noticed, and he said quickly, "Quite right, Jan. We don't put our friends in the pot, however hungry we are. You and I are friends, aren't we? And you wouldn't think of putting me in the pot. Here's some chocolate to make you fat, like me."

He put his hand in his pocket, but there was

nothing there. Then he saw that Jan was already eating the chocolate.

"Oh, it's like that, is it?" said Ivan. "I'd brought you something else as well, made it myself. But I've changed my mind. I'll keep it."

"I've got it," said Jan.

From under his seat he produced a wooden treasure box, trim and neat, with the letters JAN burned into the top.

Ivan looked so astonished that Ruth couldn't help laughing. But she was angry with Jan.

"If you don't say 'Thank you,' I'll break it," she said.

"Thank you," snapped Jan.

"You little animal," said Ruth. "It seems we shall have to leave you behind."

"Can't stop me coming," said Jan.

"You'd better take these back with you, Ivan," said Ruth. She handed him the shoes he had brought for Jan. "Please lock them up, and don't let him have them unless he apologizes."

So Ivan took them away again.

Now Jan had no shoes at all. The rags he had bound his feet with during the winter were worn out. He endured the cold and the dirt and the sharp stones underfoot for a whole week before he could bring himself to apologize. He went to the control post with cut feet, sobbing, truly repentant. He left a peace offering for Ivan — one of the treasures from his wooden box, one he prized very highly. It was a dead, shrivelled up lizard. And he came back with his shoes.

It is doubtful if Ivan valued the dead lizard as highly as Jan did. What happened to it after the boy left is Ivan's secret.

CHAPTER 11

THE ROAD
TO POSEN

SPRING was bursting when Ruth, Jan, and Bronia left Warsaw on the first stage of their long journey to Switzerland. The sun blazed from a clear sky. Birds had made their nests among the ruins (there were no trees now), and they were singing.

The children carried nothing with them except a day's food, a couple of blankets, the wooden box with the sword in it, and Jimpy the cock. Ruth had the blankets strapped to her back. Jan had the box under one arm, the cock under the other. Everything else Ruth had given to her schoolchildren.

First they called at the control post to say good-by to Ivan. But he was away, and she had to leave a message. She was sorry not to see

him personally, for he had been very kind to them.

A family group passed tugging a handcart. On it was a mangled bedstead, two drawers without a chest, a bundle of clothes, and a sleeping baby.

"Which is the way to Posen?" said Ruth.

"Follow us," they said.

The children followed them along a narrow street, between smoking rubble. No buildings were standing. The Nazis had blown everything up before they left.

When they came to a crossing, they said good-by and turned on to the main road, which led westward out of the city. It was crowded with refugees. Some were going one way, some the other, it didn't seem to matter which way as long as they kept moving. On all their faces was the same dazed look. As Ruth looked at them — the haggard old men, the bowed women, the children with gleaming eyes — there was no room in her heart for anything but pity. But they did not disturb her inward contentment, for she had hope and firmness of purpose, and she knew where she was going.

"I wish we could get a lift," said Jan. "Jimpy's tired of being carried, and he doesn't like walking."

The lorries that passed them were all full, nearly always with soldiers.

"I like walking," said Bronia. She was proud of the shoes Ivan had brought her. Very few of the refugees had shoes.

But she tired in the afternoon and was glad when a half-empty lorry came along and gave them a lift. They sat in the back, among tins of oil and petrol, and ate the food they had brought in their pockets.

They were out in the country now. The fields were littered with the debris of war — derelict tanks, shell cases, dugouts, lines and twists of rusty barbed wire. In some places peasants were digging, but most of the land had gone out of cultivation, as there was no one to attend to it.

When the lorry set them down it was evening, and they were a hundred miles on their way. Tired, grateful, and with their hopes shining, they spent the night in a derelict farm building.

"Perhaps tomorrow we shall be in Posen," said Ruth, as she snuggled under her blanket with Bronia.

"Shall we see Edek?" said Bronia.

"Yes, we shall see Edek," said Ruth. She clasped Bronia close to her, and they fell asleep.

But there were no lifts next day. All the lorries were full, and by evening they had covered only twenty miles. Bronia's feet were blistered, Jan was cross, and Jimpy was dazed with the jogging and hopping. He would not last much longer. Ruth had expected trouble with Jimpy, but she knew that if she had made Jan leave him behind Jan would not have come.

On the afternoon of the fourth day they reached Posen. The city was not as flat as Warsaw, for some of the buildings were still standing.

At the first control post Ruth produced the slip of paper that Ivan had given her, with Edek's name and address. She was directed to a large building by the river, which they had great difficulty in finding. And when at last they found it — a great sprawling barracks, with a crumbling front and a dreary courtyard — their troubles were not over. Russians had taken the place over from the Poles in the past few days, and everything was in a muddle. She went inside alone, without the children. The secretary was new and could not find the records about Edek.

"He must be here," said Ruth. "When I heard he was here, I wrote to you to say we were coming."

"There's no postal service," said the secretary.

"I sent it through the military," said Ruth.

As the secretary turned up another file, Ruth described her brother carefully.

"Did you say Edek Balicki?" said a man passing down the crowded corridor. He wore a white coat and had a stethoscope round his neck. "I sent him yesterday to the Warthe camp with the other T.B. cases."

Ruth tried to question him, but he was gone.

"The camp's only a mile down the river," said the secretary. "Won't you stay and have something to eat first? You look dreadfully tired and hungry."

But Ruth excused herself because of the two children waiting for her outside. So Edek was ill. She must press on and find him quickly.

It was dark when they crossed the bridge

and came to the gates of the Warthe camp. Ruth was carrying Bronia, who was asleep. Jan was carrying Jimpy's limp form. They could not see the buildings. Someone led them into a dimly lit hall. It was gloomy and deadly quiet, a place of sick people. Edek had always been so lively and healthy. Ruth could not imagine him belonging here.

They did not have to wait long to hear about him. There was no need to search through files. The man who spoke to them remembered Edek well.

"He was a wild boy and would not stay with us," he said, and he sounded both weary and bitter. "Edek ran away this morning. I cannot tell you where. We had no time to run after him. There are so many here who need our help. We cannot waste time on those who refuse it."

CHAPTER 12

THE HAND

THE village of Kolina lay to the north of Posen. A sandy track led to it across the fields. This track was crowded with people, many of them children, for rumor had it that a large field kitchen had arrived in the village and that a relief organization was starting work.

It was partly the thought of food and rest that sent Ruth, Bronia, and Jan there, and partly the fact that everyone was going there and they were caught up in the stream. There was no point in loafing about in Posen, and Ruth was unwilling to press on to Switzerland without Edek.

As they drew near, they were greeted by sounds of hammering, by laughter and shouting. Wooden huts were springing up all round the green. A concrete mixer was at work laying foundations, and not far away a Russian field kitchen was busy preparing food.

A relief officer divided the people into groups as they arrived. The three children were taken into a field which was roped off from the huts and crowded with youngsters, most of them sitting quietly on the ground.

"We're getting dinner ready now," they were told. "It will be your turn soon."

At the sound of a trumpet they were shepherded into a queue, which dragged its way slowly, silently, and hungrily toward the kitchens.

As they approached, Ruth caught the warm, cheering smell of soup. She watched the nearest cook, busy with his ladle, the steam from the soup urn rising up to his merry face.

"The war's over, I tell you. Our Russian armies have met the Americans on the Elbe. Germany's done for," he was saying. "Wonderful news, isn't it? I don't know what's wrong with these children. You'd think it would cheer them up to hear that the war's over, but they don't seem to hear me. You, sonny — you with the sick giraffe under your arm — oh, it's a cock, is it? looks to me a bit trodden on — aren't you glad the bombs have stopped dropping?"

But Jan's mind was on the bowl he was clasping in both hands, lifting it up to be filled.

"Here's an extra dollop for the sick pal under your arm," said the cook. "Let's hope it'll make him sit up and crow. If not, give him to me and I'll turn him into soup. He's good for a couple of mouthfuls. Next, please."

Someone slipped bread into Jan's hand, and he filed on, sipping the soup as he shuffled on past the kitchens to find a corner to sit down.

"Hey, look where you're going!" a voice cried.

Jan tripped. He fell, one hand still clutching the bowl, the other thrust out to break his fall, and Jimpy tumbling too. The bowl struck a stone and broke. The soup drained away into the dust. There were little lumps of meat and bread and vegetable lying about, still recognizable.

Up till now, the feeding had proceeded in silence. No one but the cooks and the helpers seemed to feel the need to speak.

Now, in a moment all control vanished. The sight of the spilt food was too much for the orderly queue. They burst their ranks and sprang upon it, a rabble of wildly hungry children. Jan was the center of a fighting scrimmage. Even Ruth had flung herself forward and, in spite of herself, was struggling with the rest.

As she struggled, she thought not of the food but of Bronia — what would happen to Bronia in a scrimmage like this?

The sudden onrush took the soldiers and workers by surprise. They did what they could to restore order. But it was as if a dam had burst, and all they could do was stand aside till the waters had subsided.

Jan, dirty and much bruised, was the last to pick himself up. Jimpy lay quite still, his neck broken. The boy was too dazed to grasp what had happened.

The broken bits of bowl had been squashed into the ground. Of the spilt food, there was no sign anywhere. Then a sparrow spotted a single breadcrumb and, dipping down swiftly, thieved it without anyone's noticing.

Someone took Jan by the elbow and made him sit down, placing a fresh bowl of steaming soup in his hands.

Where was Bronia?

Mercifully, she had not been in the scrimmage at all. The cook, who had been in the act of serving her, had snatched her up and held her clear. It was as well that he had, for she was the smallest person there.

And Ruth?

There had been children on top and all

round her, and someone's foot had been on her hair, so that she could not turn her head. She had reached blindly for the food but caught only a hand. For some reason or other she clung on to the hand, and when everyone about her had got up and her hair was free she had not let go. Then she looked to see whose hand it was, and it was Edek's.

CHAPTER 13

FROZEN JOURNEY

THERE was still something left of the railway station at Posen, and the track had been mended. Of course there was no such thing as a timetable; but some trains, though much delayed, were getting through to Berlin, 250 miles to the west.

In one of these trains Ruth, Edek, Jan, and Bronia were traveling. It was crowded with refugees. They leaned from the windows, stood on the footboards, lay on the carriage roofs. Ruth's family was in one of the open trucks, which was cold but not quite so crowded.

"I don't like this truck," said Bronia. "It jolts too much."

"Every jolt takes us nearer to Switzerland," said Ruth. "Think of it like that, and it's not so bad."

"There's no room to stretch."

"Rest your head against me and try and go to sleep. There, that's better."

"It's a better truck than the other ones," said Jan. "It's got a stove in it. And we can scrape the coal dust off the floor. That's why I chose it. When it gets dark, they'll light a fire and we shall keep warm."

"The stove's right in the far corner. We shan't feel it from here," said Bronia.

"Stop grumbling, Bronia," said Ruth. "We're lucky to be here at all. Hundreds of people were left behind at Posen; they may have to wait for weeks."

"Edek was lucky to come at all," said Jan. "The doctor wanted to send him back to the Warthe camp, didn't he?"

"He said you wanted fattening up, as if you were a goose being fattened for Christmas," laughed Bronia.

"The doctor wouldn't have let him come at all, if I hadn't argued with him," said Jan.

"They wanted to keep us all, didn't they, Ruth?" said Bronia.

"It was because they wanted to look after us," said Ruth. And she thought with satisfaction how they had stuck to their point and persuaded the authorities to let them go. She smiled as she remembered the conversation she had overheard afterward between the doctor and Mrs. Borowicz, the welfare officer. "Those children insist on going to Switzerland — it's their promised land — and we've no power to detain them," Mrs. Borowicz had said. And when the doctor had remarked that Edek was too ill and would die on the way, she had disagreed. "He believes his father's at the other end, waiting. Highly unlikely, of course, but there's a sort of fierce resolution about the boy — about all of them — which saves them from despair, and it's better than any medicine we can give him. Dope and drugs can't equal that. We must let them go."

Ruth looked at her brother. Bunched up against the side of the truck, he was staring out at the fields as they swept by. It was over two and a half years since she had last seen him. He was sixteen now, but did not look two and a half years older. So different from the Edek she remembered. His cheeks were pinched and hollow, his eyes as unnaturally bright as Jan's had once been, and he kept coughing. He looked as if he could go on lying there forever, without stirring. Yet at the Warthe camp they had described him as wild.

She looked at Jan. She was surprised how helpful and good-tempered he had been since

Jimpy's death in the scrimmage by the field kitchen. He had kept his sorrow to himself and not once referred to Jimpy since. Ruth could see that he was not entirely as ease with Edek yet. Did he resent his presence? There might be trouble here, for Edek must to some extent usurp the position that Jan had held, and Jan had a jealous nature.

She looked at Bronia. The child was asleep, her head in Ruth's lap, a smile on her face. Was she dreaming about the fairy story that Ruth had been telling her, the one about the princess of the Brazen Mountains? Perhaps in her dream Bronia was the princess, flying through the sky on her gray-blue wings. Then the Prince, who had searched for her seven long years, would be flying beside her, leading her to his mountain kingdom, where they would live happily ever after. Fairy stories always ended like that, and Ruth was happy to think that Bronia was still young enough to believe that it was the same in real life.

Ruth sighed. She leaned back, her head against the side of the truck, and dozed. And the train, with its long stream of trucks and carriages all crammed to bursting point with refugees, rattled and jolted on toward Berlin.

In the evening, the train stopped and was

shunted into a siding. Everyone got out to stretch his legs, but no one went far away in case it started again. As the night came on and it grew colder, they drifted back to their carriages and trucks. Coal dust was scraped from the floorboards and wood collected from outside, and the fire in Ruth's truck kindled. The refugees crowded round, stretching out their hands to the warmth.

It was the hour of the singer and the storyteller. While they all shared what little food they had, a young man sang and his wife accompanied him on the guitar. He sang of the storks that every spring fly back from Egypt to Poland's countryside, and of the villagers that welcome them by placing cartwheels on the treetops and the chimney stacks for the storks to build their nests on. A printer from Cracow told the tale of Krakus, who killed the dragon, and of Krakus' daughter, who refused to marry a German prince. Others, laughing and making light of their experiences, told of miraculous escapes from the Nazis.

"I had a free ride on the roof of a Nazi lorry," said one. "It was eighty miles before I was seen. A sniper spotted me from the top of a railway bridge, but he couldn't shoot straight and I slid off into the bushes. The driver was so un-

nerved at the shooting that he drove slap into
the bridge, and that was the end of him."

Another told of a long journey on the roof
of a train.

"I can beat that for a yarn," said Edek.

Everyone turned round to look at the boy
slumped down at the back of the truck. It was
the first time he had spoken.

"I'll tell you if you'll give me a peep at the
fire," he said. "And my sisters, too. And Jan.
We're freezing out here."

Ungrudgingly they made a way for the family — the only children in the truck — to squeeze
through to the stove. Ruth carried Bronia, who
did not wake, and she snuggled down beside
it. Jan sat on the other side, with his chin on
his knees and his arms clasping them. Edek
stood up, with his back to the side of the truck.
When someone opened the stove to throw in a
log, a shower of sparks leapt up, and for a few
moments the flames lit up his pale features.

"I was caught smuggling cheese into Warsaw,
and they sent me back to Germany to slave on
the land," he said. "The farm was near Guben
and the slaves came from all parts of Europe,
women mostly and boys of my age. In winter
we cut peat to manure the soil. We were at it
all day, from dawn to dark. In spring we did

the sowing — cabbage crop, mostly. At harvest time we packed the plump white cabbage heads in crates and sent them into town. We lived on the outer leaves — they tasted bitter. I tried to run away, but they always fetched me back. Last winter, when the war turned against the Nazis and the muddles began, I succeeded. I hid under a train, under a cattle wagon, and lay on top of the axle with my arms and legs stretched out."

"When the train started, you fell off," said Jan.

"Afterward I sometimes wished I had," said Edek, "that is, until I found Ruth and Bronia again. Somehow I managed to cling on, and I got a free ride back to Poland."

Jan laughed scornfully. "Why don't you travel that way here? It would leave the rest of us more room."

"I could never do that again," said Edek.

"No," said Jan, and he looked with contempt at Edek's thin arms and bony wrists. "You're making it all up. There's no room to lie under a truck. Nothing to hold on to."

Edek seized him by the ear and pulled him to his feet. "Have you ever looked under a truck?" he said, and he described the underside in such convincing detail that nobody but Jan would have questioned his accuracy. The boys were coming to blows, when the printer pulled Jan to the floor and there were cries of, "Let him get on with his story!"

"You would have been shaken off," Jan shouted above the din, "like a rotten plum!"

"That's what anyone would expect," Edek shouted back. "But if you'll shut up and listen, I'll tell you why I wasn't." When the noise had died down, he went on. "Lying on my stomach, I found the view rather monotonous. It made me dizzy too. I had to shut my eyes. And the bumping! Compared with that, the boards of this truck are like a featherbed. Then the train ran through a puddle. More than a puddle — it must have been a flood, for I was splashed and soaked right through. But that water saved me. After that I couldn't let go, even if I'd wanted to."

"Why not?" said Jan, impressed.

"The water froze on me. It made an icicle of me. When at last the train drew into a station, I was encased in ice from head to foot. I could hear Polish voices on the platform. I knew we must have crossed the frontier. My voice was the only part of me that wasn't frozen, so I shouted. The stationmaster came and chopped me down with an ax. He wrapped me in blankets and carried me to the boiler-house to thaw out. Took me hours to thaw out."

"You don't look properly thawed out yet," said the printer, and he threw him a crust of bread.

Other voices joined in. "Give him a blanket." "A tall story, but he's earned a bed by the stove." "Another story, somebody! One to make us forget." "Put some romance in it."

The stories petered out after a while. When all was quiet, and the refugees, packed like sardines on the floor of the truck, lay sleeping under the cold stars, Ruth whispered to Edek, "Was it really true?"

"Yes, it was true," said Edek.

"Nothing like that must ever happen to you again," said Ruth.

She reached for his hand — it was cold, although he was close to the stove — and she clasped it tight, as if she meant never to let go of it again.

CHAPTER 14

CITY OF THE LOST

I T was the end of May when the train reached Berlin — after nine days of stopping and starting, of lying up in sidings, of crawling along the battered track.

The station was a shambles, but everyone was glad to escape from their cramped quarters. They swarmed out of the trucks and over the lines, some of them disappearing at once into the dusty ruins of Berlin. Most of them hung about or sat down on their luggage — hundreds of tired and disconsolate men, women, and children — in the hope that they would be given food or told where to go. A few UNRRA workers appeared, shouting orders in broken German, trying to make them stand in a queue. Carts piled with bread pushed their way through the mob, and there was some ladling of milk out of vats for the mothers and babies. But this was the second refugee train that had come in that day, and there was not enough food to go round.

Hungry and unfed, the family were directed to a transit camp not far away. They left the station shouting and laughing, for their spirits were high. Only a few weeks ago they were in Warsaw; ten days ago Edek had not been found; and now they were all together and had covered a third of the way to Switzerland.

They did not seem to notice that everything around them had been destroyed, that buildings which had stood for generations had been wiped out. Perhaps it was because they were too used to it — Warsaw looked no different. Perhaps it was because the sun was shining, the birds were singing, and Switzerland was just around the corner.

"Nobody's going hungry," said Jan, and from the mischievous grin on his face Ruth knew that he was about to show them he had not lost his gift for sleight of hand. Out of his shirt popped a long cigar-shaped loaf of bread. They all sprang to catch it, but Jan held it high above his head and ran across the road.

There was a blaring of horn, a screeching of

brakes, and a jeep grazed his pants. A voice shouted some insult at him in a language he did not understand.

Turning, Jan looked up into the mustache of a British officer. He made a long nose at it and in a leisurely manner finished his crossing of the street.

The officer pretended not to notice and waved his driver on.

Each party promptly dismissed the matter from his mind. But they were to meet again soon — and in the oddest of circumstances.

Meanwhile all interest was focused upon the loaf. The four sat down in the rubble to make short work of it.

"I bet it cost you a pretty penny," said Edek, sarcastically.

"I *borrowed* it when the cart came round," said Jan.

"In Germany we call that 'organizing,'" said Edek.

There was more food for them at the transit camp, a disused cinema whose floor appeared to contain the entire population of Berlin. After four helpings of soup each, they were given blankets and straw-filled mattresses and ushered into a dark corner of the hall. Here a seedy-looking flag and a scribbled notice on the wall

indicated that they were in "Poland." The electricity was not working, and the only light came
from hurricane lamps suspended from the balcony above.

As far as they could see, the whole floor was
carpeted with mattresses. They threw down
theirs where they stood — in the no-man's-land
between "Poland" and "Yugoslavia."

This was to be their home while they were
in Berlin. It was warm and dry and comfortable,
and they were delighted — especially Bronia,
who loved to hear Polish voices, as they made
it feel like home. Next to her she found a child
of her own age, whose mother was as good as
Ruth at telling stories and knew many folk tales
that Bronia had never heard.

In spite of the crowded conditions, all was
quiet and orderly in the hall. Except at meal
times, when they went up on to the balcony,
people were content to lie about on their mattresses, smoking, reading, talking, playing cards.
The night was so quiet that Edek felt ashamed
of his coughing and tried to smother it in his
blanket for fear of waking the sleepers.

Then, in the early morning, when the first
wakers were stirring, came an unexpected moment of panic.

Someone shrieked near the entrance. People

sat up, heaved off their blankets, stood up, craned their necks to see what was happening. There was a general movement toward the entrance, stifled almost at once by another in the opposite direction. A wave of bodies rolled inward, and for a minute or two it looked as if there were going to be a stampede. Then, as abruptly as it had begun, the noise died down and all was quiet again.

"What was it all about?" said Bronia.

"Here's somebody who can tell us," said Ruth, as an excited new arrival, jumping from mattress to mattress, landed three jumps away.

"A chimpanzee escaped from the zoo!" the new arrival announced breathlessly.

Jan was instantly alert. "That's nothing to be afraid of," he said. "I wish he'd come over here."

"Thank the Lord the brute's taken itself off," said the man.

"Oh," said Jan. If he had been told that Switzerland had been flattened in an earthquake, he could not have been more disappointed.

"Those Greeks threw their boots at it and a couple of hurricane lamps as well. They've got some sense."

"Stupid," said Jan. "The chimpanzee will copy them, and someone will get hurt."

He was ready to continue the argument, but

the Pole on the mattress opposite was reading out (or rather, translating) from a German news sheet an article that demanded all his attention.

"Chimpanzee escapes from zoo," he translated. "At large since Monday evening. Bistro the chimpanzee, who for some years has delighted visitors to the Tiergarten with his amusing antics, escaped from his cage on Monday night. He was seen to board a tram in the Adolf Hitler Strasse, where he bit one of the terrified passengers before alighting at the next stop. Police gave chase, but the animal climbed a derelict building and, from a dangerous perch high above the street, proceeded to throw bricks at anyone who approached. He was still there when darkness fell. A watch was kept on the building all night. But the animal must have given them the slip, for he was not there in the morning. There have been several reports of him since, many of them contradictory."

The reader looked up from the news sheet and saw with some surprise that all Poland was standing on his mattress. Flattered, he continued, "Bistro was one of the few animals to escape unhurt from the bombing of the Tiergarten. A highly intelligent and usually docile animal, with a passion for cigarettes, he appears to have been much shaken by the months of bombing the city has endured. His keeper reports that he has been difficult to handle because of his melancholy and sometimes violent moods. Anyone who sees him is advised to do nothing to anger him and to report at once to the police."

The crowd dispersed, and the news sheet passed from hand to hand. Soon, somewhat the worse for wear, it disappeared into Yugoslavia.

"It's a good thing Bistro took himself off," said Ruth, who had returned to her mattress.

"Jan would have saved us if he hadn't," said Bronia.

"Where *is* Jan?" asked Edek.

Jan's mattress was uninhabited. They looked for him, but he had vanished.

CHAPTER 15

JAN FINDS
A NEW PAL

LATER that week, in the sitting room of a Berlin house which had been commandeered for him, a British officer was writing home to his wife. It was the officer whose jeep had so nearly knocked Jan over outside the station.

"Dearest Jane," he wrote. "My unit's been in Berlin a week now — we're here to meet the Russians. You never saw such a place. Other cities were badly blitzed, but not on this scale. I've seen pictures of it as it used to be — one of the world's great capitals. Now it's more like a moon landscape — craters everywhere, mountains of rubble. The Reichstag and the Kaiser's Palace are roofless; Unter den Linden is piled with wreckage. And the queerest things keep happening. How's this for one? I've been attacked by a chimpanzee! Don't worry — I'm quite O.K., not hurt at all.

"On Wednesday I was sitting in the jeep with my driver, studying a map. I had a cigarette in my mouth and was about to light it when a hand slid over my shoulder, clapped on my lips, and tweaked the cigarette out. I looked round and saw a chimpanzee jumping up and down on the back seat, with the cigarette in his mouth. You never saw such a revolting creature — huge arms, hairy chest as broad as mine, deep-set evil eyes, and the face of a heavyweight boxer. He could have knocked the pair of us into the middle of next month, but we didn't stay to let him. We streaked out the door and left him to his dancing.

"Quite a crowd was gathering — they kept their distance, of course — and I heard someone say the chimp was called Bistro and he'd escaped from the zoo, or what was left of it after the bombing. He had a chain round his neck, and it kept clanking against the tailboard as he jumped. He seemed to be in a rage because he hadn't any matches, or because he'd swallowed the cigarette and it was making his belly ache. When he was tired of jumping, he sat down in the driver's seat and started fiddling with the controls.

"That put the wind up me. There was a good-ish slope on the street, and fifty yards ahead a bomb crater big enough to swallow a church — and cordoned off with only a bit of rope and a plank or two. If the jeep took a header down there, I should be answerable.

" 'Come on, Jim,' I said to my driver. 'We'll have to do something about this.' But my knees were like jelly, and I think Jim's were too.

"Then the strangest thing happened. A boy stepped out of the crowd, one of the thousands of urchins that abound in the ruins here — about eleven or twelve years old, I should say, but you can never tell with these kids, they're so undernourished.

"I shouted to him in German to come back, but he didn't understand. He was a Pole and his name was Jan, though I didn't know that till afterward. But I recognized him as a boy we'd nearly run down in the street the day before.

"He walked right on, quite unafraid, and when he was alongside the jeep he said in a gentle voice, 'Hello, Bistro.'

"The chimp gave him a dirty look, but Jan only grinned. He fished something out of a small wooden box he was carrying, and it made the chimp curious. It was a cigarette and matches. He handed over the cigarette. Then the matches.

"'OOOO, Warro . . . umph,' said Bistro, and he lit up at once and flung away the matches. He sat back in the driver's seat, inhaling, puffing out clouds of smoke from his nose, and all the while keeping his eyes fixed on Jan. Quite suddenly Bistro stood up and held out a soft pink-palmed hand for the boy to shake. Then he climbed over on to the back seat and lay down, his legs crossed, and puffed away.

"It may have been my imagination, but I swear that the jeep began to move. Like a fool, I tiptoed up behind and called out in my best German, 'Sonny, put the brake on; she's begin-

ning to shift.' He didn't understand. I panto-
mimed the action.

"But Bistro didn't like me. He sat up and
screamed. Then he opened the toolbox, which
Jim had been farsighted enough to leave on the
floor, and flung the wheel brace at me. It made
him mad to see me duck, so he generously made
me a present of the whole toolbox plus contents
in one almighty fling. It hit the pavement, scat-
tering the crowd. Out of the corner of my eye
I saw him leap over the back and shoot after me.

"I don't know what happened next. I ran for
my life; it was all rubble and dust and scramble
up here and slide down there. I ran behind a
wall, panting. Then I realized I wasn't being
followed any more, and I heard the boy's shrill
voice, scolding.

"I peeped out, down into the street.

"The boy had got a stick from somewhere
and was standing with it raised above his head.
Bistro lay in the dust at his feet, his face and
head covered with his long arms, whimpering.
I don't know whether the boy had struck him
or not. I expect not, for I guess it would have
been as effective as trying to knock down the
Eiffel Tower with a flyswatter. But there was
no doubt about the scolding he gave. When it
was all over, Bistro sat up cautiously and started

to pick a few fleas out of his chest and eat them. He offered one to Jan as a peace offering.

"Then Bistro did something to Jan that would have killed me dead of fright if I'd been in his place. He took the boy's hand in his, lifted it to his mouth, and bit his finger. Jan stood as still as a rock. Some sixth sense which most people don't possess must have whispered to him what the chimp was up to. It wasn't a real bite, only a nip — and a token of friendship between the two. So the keeper explained afterward. When Bistro gave his hand to the boy in return, Jan knew what to do. He gave it a friendly nip with his teeth.

"Next thing I knew, Jan was leading him down the street by the chain. Only Bistro didn't wear it like a prisoner's chain, but with pride and glory, as if it were a chain of office.

"That's not quite the end of the story. Jim had fixed up the jeep and braked it properly. Now he was picking up the scattered tools, and I saw he had the boy's wooden box, too. I strolled over to help him — or rather, to direct operations, as it doesn't do for an officer to go down on his hands and knees. I felt a fool in front of all those people. I knew they were laughing at me.

"Then I saw a small silver sword, sort of

paper knife, lying in the dust. It hardly looked worth bothering about, but I got Jim to pick it up.

"Two keepers had arrived by now and were leading Bistro away. We found Jan, and Jim handed him his wooden box. Seeing the lid was loose, the boy checked through the contents in great agitation, then burst into tears. I tried to ask him what was the matter; then I remembered the silver sword and, showing it to him, asked him if he'd lost it. The cloudburst ended abruptly, and out came the sun again. He seized it greedily, wrapped it up, and popped it into the box amongst the other treasures. It didn't seem to me worth all the fuss he made, but evidently he attached some importance to it.

"I invited Jan round to my lodgings for dinner — he looked as if he hadn't had a square meal since he was born — and he turned up promptly with three other Polish children as skinny as himself. Luckily Frau Schmidt's larder with its army rations was equal to the occasion. One of them, a sixteen-year-old lad named Edek, with a cough like a deep-sea foghorn, spoke some German, so I learned all about them.

"They're on their way to Switzerland to find their parents — started from Warsaw last month — and they don't mind footing it all the way if they have to. Jan doesn't really belong at all. Ruth, the eldest (about seventeen), picked him up on a slagheap half dead and adopted him. She's a remarkable girl, quiet and self-assured, with the most striking eyes — they have a deep serenity, a sense of purpose and moral authority quite unmistakable. No wonder they look up to her as a mother and a leader, too.

"Edek is brave and intelligent, and looks as if he had suffered a lot. He spent nearly two years slaving for the Nazis. You can see it in his face — a kid's face oughtn't to be creased and pinched like his. I wonder if he'll hold out. Switzerland's a long way.

"The one that took my fancy most was Bronia, the youngest. Blue eyes, very fair hair, she seemed to live in a dream world — like our own Jenny, as I remember her on my last leave. I didn't understand a word Bronia said and she didn't understand a word I said, but we got on fine together. If they don't find what they're looking for in Switzerland — and I'm afraid it may be only a mirage — I was wondering if perhaps we . . . But it's no use thinking that way. I'm sure Ruth wouldn't part with the child, and quite right, too.

"I scrounged some clothes and army rations for them, and they left in the afternoon, singing at the top of their voices. It went right to my heart. Tomorrow they start on the next stage of their long journey. 750 miles. . . .

"That's all, dear. More next week.

"My love to you, and a special hug for Jenny.

MARK

"P.S. Frau Schmidt had the cheek to wake me up in the night to tell me some of her silver was missing, and she accused those Polish children. I couldn't have cared less. They could have walked off with half the house for all I minded. Really, these Germans! They spend five years looting Europe and then come crying to you in the middle of the night because someone's pinched a jam spoon.

"We found the missing silver in the letterbox next morning. I bet my bottom dollar it was Jan who pinched it — you never saw such a mischievous face — and Ruth who made him take it back. She's got as firm a hold over that family as Jan had over the chimp."

CHAPTER 16

THROUGH THE
RUSSIAN ZONE

"TAKE the Potsdam road and follow your noses," the family were told, and off they went, singing a gay song, with their heads in the air. If they had gone due west toward Belgium, they might have traveled more quickly, for this was the general direction of the traffic. Fewer refugees were moving south, so lifts were scarce and they were on their feet most of the time.

They crossed the Elbe near Rosslau by a bridge that had not been too badly damaged for the Russians to repair. Here they were held up for half a day by a spearhead of the Russian army, bound (so rumor had it) for Prague to drive the Germans out of Czechoslovakia.

Never before had Ruth seen so many soldiers.

First came the tanks to clear the way. Next, column after column of marching soldiers, tired and dirty in their ragged uniforms. They came from the Ukraine and the Tartar republics, from the Ural mountains and the Caucasus, from the countries of the Baltic, from Siberia, Mongolia. Over the bridge they poured in their thousands, while everyone else stood by to let them pass.

"I know that song," cried Bronia, as she caught a snatch of a Cossack song from a group of soldiers. "Father taught it to us. Do you remember?"

"Yes, I remember," said Ruth. "It was the summer we spent by the Dunajec River. We were on a raft, floating downstream between the wooded peaks."

She sighed, and the tune was lost in another burst of singing. Standing there, they heard many songs, some of them bright and jolly, some of them slow and poignantly sad.

The family squeezed over the bridge behind the last of the marching columns.

They were hardly across when screaming horns announced the arrival of the staff cars, mostly Mercedeses and Horchs which had been taken from the Nazis. Next, cars with secretaries; cars with war booty — fur coats, textiles, carpets, looted china; lorries with furniture, radios, refrigerators; food lorries with tons and tons of Russian delicacies — caviar, sturgeon, vodka, Crimean wine; lorries bearing proud posters: WE WELCOME THE LIBERATING ARMY.

More marching columns.

Columns of women and girls in gray-green uniform, with tight blouses and high boots. They had come to do the cooking and washing, to help in the hospitals and look after the sick. Tagged on to them were clusters of small boys picked up from the woods and burned-out villages. They had come because they were hungry and the Red Army was ready to feed them.

"The whole world's gone by today. Surely there can't be any more people left?" said Bronia, as the dust began to subside.

But there was still the rearguard to come, and soon the dust was flying again under the wheels of hundreds of small light carts drawn by low Cossack horses.

"Now for a lift!" cried Jan, as a gray old man, whip in hand, came rattling by in a cart with a canvas roof. And before Ruth could stop him, he had hauled himself up over the tailboard.

"We'll never catch him up — the carts are all full," cried Ruth.

But soon an open cart, with nothing in the

back but a heap of straw, some fodder, and a leg of smoked pork picked up the three of them. It was an anxious ride, for the cart was traveling more slowly than Jan's, and what with the dust and the overtaking and the spreading out into the fields on either side of the road they quickly lost sight of Jan.

Jan was perfectly happy. He had landed on a pile of straw as comfortable as a featherbed, beside a sick soldier and a pen with a squawking goose. And if it was not worth his while to make the acquaintance of the soldier, he thought quite differently about the goose.

All afternoon Ruth and Edek kept a lookout for Jan's cart. As it happened, their vigilance proved unnecessary, for the whole caravan halted at dusk to camp for the night. Fires were kindled, stock replenished from nearby farms, and there was eating and drinking and singing. Jan was quickly found and forgiven.

Next day their ways parted, and the family cut across country in the direction of Bitterfield and Halle.

Before they left Berlin, the British officer had provided them with ration cards, and with the money he had given them they were able to buy food. For recapturing the chimp Jan had been rewarded with a hundred marks. He entrusted this to Ruth and did not question how she chose to spend it. When at last the money ran out, they were dependent on what they could beg or work for. Work was difficult to find, for the factories were idle and farms had absorbed the first prisoners of war to be released. Some villages refused to admit them, having neither food nor shelter for any more refugees. But for the most part they met with kindness and were not refused food if it could be spared.

Most big towns had their UNRRA food kitchens, and these were always welcome. But best of all were the transit camps. It was the time when camp commandants used to send soldiers round with guns to seize stores. They ransacked warehouses, factories, shops, even garrets and barns, for the peasants had hidden plenty away and the slave workers that swelled the camps often knew the hiding places. One such camp had a Polish section, where a school had been started. Had the family stayed here — and they were pressed to do so — they would have received all the food and schooling and medical attention that they needed. Edek was very tired when they arrived, and Ruth was ready to stay as long as he needed rest. But he recovered after a few days and was eager to be off. Whenever he was tempted to linger, one peep at the silver sword was enough to spur him on again.

All day long the sun smiled down upon them; upon toilers in the fields where fresh crops were springing up; upon towns littered with the debris of war; upon a people numbed by defeat, living from day to day, with no thought for the future; upon women standing in bread queues or wheeling barrows of wood they had collected in the forest for their kitchen fires; upon wounded soldiers sitting on hospital balconies, basking in the sun's heat. Some of the soldiers waved to the family as they passed by, and the family waved back.

So they came to the edge of the Russian zone.

In the early days of peace, there were many places where it was not difficult to slip unobserved from one zone to the next. They crossed the frontier somewhere in the Thuringian forest, without realizing that they had done so, and it was only the unfamiliar uniforms of the soldiers and the strange language of the notices that told them they had now reached the American zone.

CHAPTER 17

THE SIGNAL

IT was the middle of June. In spite of the long spell of unbroken weather, Edek was no better. At night, as they lay under the bright stars, his cough would keep Ruth awake and she could not throw off her anxiety. Each day his walking became slower and more painful. This was partly because his feet were sore, for his shoes had worn out and the substitute pair he had plaited from reeds had not lasted long. Ruth decided he must rest for a week.

They found a pleasant site in a meadow by a millstream. They planned to camp here till she and Jan had earned enough money to buy Edek a new pair of shoes. Ruth took a cleaning job at the local school, while Jan went hay-making. And Edek rested under the trees, with Bronia to look after him. All day he lay in the shade, for the sun was scorching hot. At night a chill wind blew; but he was warm, for they had lit a fire for him, and he lay beside it, looking up at the stars that peeped between the willow branches, till he was lulled to sleep by the gentle music of the stream.

So he rested well — and ate well too, for there was no shortage of food. Several times Jan came home from work with a bag full of such food as they had never tasted before — chicken, lobster, salted pork, and luncheon meat. When Ruth asked where it came from, he said, "From the farmer. He's a generous man." But her suspicions were not quieted, for it was all in tins and labeled in a strange language.

"I know he's stealing it," she told Edek. "It's American food, and I think he must get it from the depot. Yet I don't know — the depot is closely guarded, and I've never seen him anywhere near. If he's thieving, he'll get caught. The Americans don't miss much. There's a hall next to the school, and a military court trying cases all day long."

"He brought nothing back yesterday, or the day before," said Edek. "Perhaps the source has dried up."

"He says the farmer has promised him more tomorrow," said Ruth.

Edek was determined to clear up the mystery.

Without saying a word to Ruth, the next afternoon he went alone to the farm where Jan worked and hid behind a hedge. He saw Jan leave the hay-making before the day's work was over. Instead of returning to camp, he hurried off in the opposite direction, straight through the town.

Edek followed him to a level crossing outside the town. Suddenly a ragged youth sprang out of a bush by the roadside and beckoned to Jan. The meeting seemed to have been arranged, for Jan showed no surprise and slipped down from the road to join the youth.

Edek crept as close as he could without making his presence known and waited. He waited so long that he began to wonder if they had given him the slip.

Then suddenly Jan broke out of the cover and ran half doubled up, along one side of the railway line in the direction of the signal ramp. The youth had disappeared.

Edek climbed into a tree which gave a good view of the line. From here he saw Jan swarm up the side of the signal ramp — it extended right across the track — and lie down flat and motionless on top, above the line. What was he up to now? As far as Edek knew, train-wrecking was not one of Jan's pastimes, for in spite of his twisted sense of values he was not deliberately destructive.

"I must go and find out," thought Edek. And, jumping down from the tree, he walked along beside the track till he came to the foot of the ramp.

"What's the game, Jan?" he called.

Jan was startled, for he was still lying flat and hardly visible, and had not noticed him. He swore at Edek and told him to go away.

With a clank and rattle of loose metal that took them both by surprise, the signal on the "up" line changed to green.

"Go away, you fool, go away!" Jan screamed at him. And, flinging himself at the signal, he began to tug at it.

Edek was really agitated now, for he could hear the distant rumble of an approaching train. He shouted to Jan to come down, but the boy was working furiously with a wrench and what looked like a pair of wire cutters, and paid no heed.

The noise of the train grew louder. Puffs of dirty smoke rose above the trees.

With the thought of some dreadful accident impending, Edek sprang up the side of the ramp and started to climb.

It was not an exercise for which he was well

fitted. He had already spent most of his small reserves of strength, and his muscles were too flabby to give him much grip. The ramp, too, had been badly damaged and hastily and inexpertly repaired. An iron stanchion broke away under his foot. Gasping and coughing, with a great effort he hung on with his hands and somehow hauled himself up.

When his head appeared over the top, he saw that the signal had changed to red. Jan was slithering backward like an eel in a frantic hurry. His feet scraped past Edek's face, nearly knocking him off. As he passed him, his eyes were blazing, his face purple with fury. But because of the din of the train Edek could not hear what he said.

With no thought in his head but to prevent an accident, Edek groped his way along the top of the ramp. As the train — it was a goods train — approached, laboriously chugging, with an endless winding line of trucks, he tottered upright and waved. He need not have done so, for the signal was at red, where Jan had put it, and the engine had already started to jam the brakes on.

With a great clanking from truck to truck as the bumpers collided, the train screeched to a standstill. A hiss of steam. A long shrill

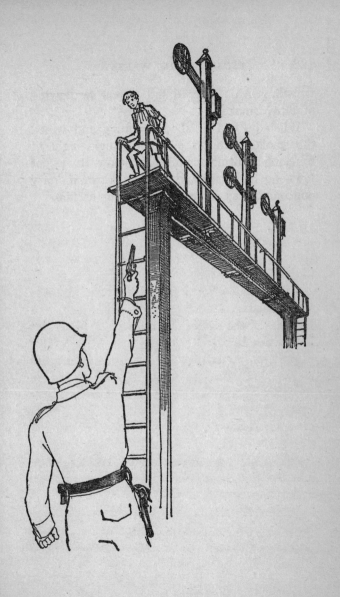

whistling. A dark cloud and a great swallowing of filthy smoke.

When he had finished coughing and wiped the smoke from his eyes, he caught sight of someone shouting at him from below. It was not Jan — he had vanished. An American military policeman was pointing a revolver at him.

CHAPTER 18

CAPTAIN GREENWOOD

CAPTAIN Greenwood of the American Army of Occupation, aged forty-two and already gray at the temples, was a lawyer in his home town. His experience fitted him well for his present role of trying petty cases. He went to great trouble to be just. This was seldom easy, as nothing was straightforward in this foreign country, and the need for using interpreters made the hearing of evidence a slow business.

The boy before him was a strange case: Edek Balicki, sixteen, a Pole, of no address, caught interfering with train signals. The prosecutor, Lieutenant James, claimed that he was one of a gang of train robbers and had been seen halting a train. The boy admitted having halted the train, but denied the rest of the charge. As nobody else had been caught and the suspected attempt to rob the train had been abandoned, the whole case could not be proved. The attempt to connect him with a previous train robbery had broken down for lack of evidence. Pressed to give some reason for his action, Edek replied that it was a prank.

Captain Greenwood was puzzled. The boy was obviously ill and did not look the sort to delight in pranks of that nature. Moreover, his refusal to have anyone to defend him did not make matters any easier.

There was a sudden stir at the back of the court, and a corporal came forward with a message for the judge. After a few moment of whispered conversation, Captain Greenwood said, "Sure — if they can help us. Show them in."

Ruth, Jan, and Bronia were shown in and made to stand beside Edek. Bronia was holding Ruth's hand and grinning happily. Jan was biting his lip. His eyes were defiant.

"There's been a mistake, and I've come to explain," said Ruth in Polish. "This is Jan. It's all his fault. I want to speak for him."

The interpreter translated.

"Who is the other child?" said the captain.

"My sister Bronia," said Ruth. "She has nothing to do with this, but I had to bring her along, as I've nowhere to leave her. We're on our way to Switzerland and are camping by the mill-stream."

"I see. What's the boy's full name?" said Captain Greenwood.

"Only Jan — that's the only name of his we know," said Ruth.

"Jan, have you any parents?" said Captain Greenwood.

"The gray cat and Jimpy, but they're dead, and Ruth's my mother now," said Jan, sullenly.

Captain Greenwood could make nothing of this. Ruth did her best to explain a situation she did not fully understand herself.

"We take it then that you have no parents, but that this young lady, Ruth Balicki, aged eighteen, sister of Edek Balicki, is your guardian," said Captain Greenwood. "You claim that Edek Balicki is wrongly accused. Lieutenant James here will read the charge and it will be translated for you. Listen carefully, Jan, and then answer our questions."

The charge of halting the train and attempted robbery were read and the prisoner was asked, "Guilty or not guilty?"

Jan's answer was to make a bolt for the door, where two guards seized him and brought him back, kicking and biting.

The judge spoke severely, but without effect. He turned to Ruth. "Have *you* any control over the boy?"

"He's scared of the soldiers," said Ruth. "If you'd kindly send those guards outside, sir, I think he'd behave himself."

Captain Greenwood gasped. This was not a request that he had met with before. But one glance at the struggle in front of him convinced him that extraordinary measures were justifiable. He told the guards to release the prisoner and wait outside the door. Jan collapsed on the floor, panting and angry, his eyes flashing.

Captain Greenwood waited for him to calm down, then asked him to stand up. To his surprise the boy obeyed.

"We are here to know the truth," he said, abandoning all formality. "Now, Jan, will you tell us in your own words what happened?"

Jan looked round the court suspiciously. Except for the lieutenant and the judge, there were no soldiers there — only the interpreter (a civilian), Edek, Bronia, and Ruth. This gave him some of the confidence he needed. He looked at Ruth.

She smiled at him; but if her smile was an encouragement to him to speak out, her words were a warning.

"Jan, no hanky-panky," she said. "If you try that, you know what you'll get."

Jan tried to see what she was holding behind her back, but he had to guess. With lowered eyes, he addressed the judge: "It's not Edek's fault. I changed the signal and he came to stop me. I ran away and he was caught. He needn't have been caught, but he's very stupid for a boy of his age. He makes a mess of everything."

"What made you want to stop the train?" said Captain Greenwood.

"The food trucks."

"You were going to raid them yourself?"

"No."

"You were one of a gang?"

"Yes."

"Was Edek Balicki a member?"

"No. He had nothing to do with the business."

"Who are the others?"

"You mean the train robbers? I never met any of them and I don't know anything about them. If I did, I wouldn't tell. Those soldiers outside can go and sniff them out."

Ruth produced a stick from behind her back and gave Jan a good clout with it on the rear. "That's for being rude," she said.

The clout had the desired effect, and he apologized.

Captain Greenwood asked Lieutenant James, who had been prosecuting Edek, if he wished to cross-examine Jan.

With a self-important flourish of his papers, the lieutenant said that he did. He clearly thought that Captain Greenwood was taking too much upon himself. He had never cared for his superior's informal ways. Clearing his throat a trifle too loudly, he leaned toward Jan. "What did this gang pay you for your services?"

"Nothing."

"You ask me to believe that you undertook this dangerous task for nothing?"

"Of course. There was nothing to give me. The train wasn't robbed. But the other times —"

Jan bit his lip. In his unusual role of honesty he had let his tongue run away with him.

"Would you explain what you mean by 'the other times'?" said Lieutenant James.

"They gave me a share of the food they took. And jolly good stuff it was."

"Except for that fat ham," put in Bronia. "That made us all sick . . . Ow!" she cried, as Ruth rapped her over the knuckles.

Lieutenant James ignored the interruption. "I see. They gave you some of the loot. But you said just now that you had never met any of them. How could they give you food without your seeing them?"

"They're a lot smarter than you think, Lieutenant," said Jan. "They left it for me in a hiding place in the wood."

"How many times did this happen?"

"Twice."

At this point Captain Greenwood intervened. "You are going beyond the terms of the charge, Lieutenant James. Nothing will be gained by pursuing this line any further now."

"With respect, sir, I —"

"Are you satisfied that the prisoner is guilty of the charge you have brought?"

"Perfectly."

"Then we can leave the matter at that. Have you no further relevant questions to put?"

"No, sir," barked the lieutenant, banging his papers on the desk. And he sat down.

Captain Greenwood turned to Jan and spoke gently. "Why do you go in for stealing when you can get plenty to eat at the food kitchens?"

"We can't live otherwise," said Jan bitterly.

"It has become a habit, a bad habit," said Captain Greenwood.

"The Nazis stole everything from our country and left us with nothing," said Jan. "Now it is our turn to steal from them."

"But this is American food you have been stealing, not Nazi food. It is sent here to feed you and all the other refugees that are flooding the country. If you steal it, you are robbing your own people. Do you think that is right or sensible?"

"I want to feed Ruth and Bronia and Edek," said Jan fiercely, and the Captain's unexpected gentleness brought the tears rolling down his cheeks. "Edek is ill, and we are all hungry. I shall always steal if they are hungry."

"Do *they* steal?"

"No. They are not as clever as I am. But everybody else does, even the Americans. They take cameras and glasses from the Germans. There are a hundred cases of wine in your canteen, all stolen. I know where they got it from."

"Those are not proper observations," said Captain Greenwood. "It won't help your case to bandy wild accusations of that sort. If there's any truth in them, they'll be brought to my notice and dealt with in the correct way."

Ruth slipped an arm round Jan's shoulders and whispered something as he fought to choke back the sobs.

Jan fumbled for an apology. At last he said, "I speak with respect, sir," a phrase which, coming from his lips, sounded so comic that the Captain could not help smiling.

"When I was your age, Jan, I was brought up on the Ten Commandments. Maybe they're out of fashion now. One of them is 'Thou shalt not steal' — ever heard of it?"

"It doesn't work," said Jan.

"It must be made to work, or everything will go to pieces. Don't forget that."

Captain Greenwood shuffled the papers on his desk, summed up briefly, and passed sentence. "Edek Balicki, not guilty, case dismissed. Jan has pleaded guilty. Under the circumstances I shall deal with him as lightly as I can. Two hundred marks' fine or seven days."

There was a brief consultation between Ruth and Jan. Then Ruth spoke: "Jan says he'll take the detention. We haven't enough money to pay the fine."

"We're saving up to buy a pair of boots for Edek," put in Bronia.

"Thank you, sir," said Ruth.

"It isn't long, Jan, and you'll be looked after," said Captain Greenwood. "When you come out, stick to that mother, as she's old enough not to have forgotten what decent behavior is." As an afterthought he added, "Remind her to send me a post card when you get to Switzerland."

He cleared the court.

Ruth held Jan's hand tightly till the guards came for him and led him away. He went without a struggle, not daring to look back at her. When he had gone, she gave one hand to Edek and one to Bronia, and they walked slowly out.

Alone in the courtroom, with a sigh Captain Greenwood turned over his notes of the morning's cases, ready to draw up the reports for his senior officer. Three cases of theft, two of failure to observe curfew, an old man accused of concealing a Storm Trooper in his house, and lastly Jan's case. It troubled him more than all the other cases put together.

As he reflected on the punishment he had given the boy, he realized that for all his noble intentions, he had only been scratching on the surface of a problem he could not begin to solve. A week's detention would not prevent Jan from stealing again. Could Ruth prevent him? She was a remarkable girl, and if anybody could help him it was she. But after five years of war and twisted living, such cases were too often beyond remedy.

CHAPTER 19

THE BAVARIAN FARMER

THERE were queer noises in the barn, louder than the scurrying of rats or the creaking of rusty hinges in the wind.

The farmer flung the door open and shouted, "Come out of there, you young devil! I heard you — can't you imitate a rat better than that?"

He stood still, accustoming his eyes to the half-darkness of the barn. The sun rose early enough in July, but it was not full daylight yet and all he could see was a vague blur of hay. While he listened, everything was so quiet that he began to wonder if he had been mistaken.

Then the sound of a half-sob, stifled immediately, confirmed his suspicions.

"Come out!" he shouted. "Do I smoke you out like rabbits or fetch the prong?"

The threats were ineffective, so he went off to fetch the prong. Soon the hay was flying.

And something else came flying too — an over-ripe turnip, which, beautifully aimed, struck the farmer full in the nape of the neck. He swore.

An anxious voice piped up, "We give in — please put that horrible thing away before it goes right through Bronia." And the farmer turned round, his prong poised in mid-air, to find himself face to face with a tall, thin girl, her clothes and hair bristling with bits of hay. "We only spent the night here. We haven't done any harm."

When she realized that he had not properly understood, Ruth called Edek.

The hay at the farmer's feet parted, and Edek's spluttering face appeared. He had held his breath all too long and made a dive for the open air, clinging to the handle of the barn door while he coughed the chaff out of his lungs.

"Hey, that's me you're stepping on!" shrilled Bronia, as she emerged from under the farmer's left foot. And when she saw the murderous prong, she flew to Ruth and hid behind her.

"Edek, tell him we only spent the night here and we haven't done any harm," said Ruth, with one arm round Bronia.

Edek translated.

"No harm!" exclaimed the farmer, removing a splodgy mess from inside his shirt collar. "I suppose you call this a birthday present. One — two — three of you. Is that the lot, or have we another batch lurking somewhere?"

The reply was another wet turnip. It landed on exactly the same spot as before. The last member of the family, who was certainly no diplomat, had launched his second missile. Now he came sliding down from the top of the hay, for no other reason than that he had run out of ammunition.

Bronia giggled, Edek grinned, but Ruth was angry.

"When will you grow up, you silly little boy!" she said, seizing him by the shoulders and shaking him like a puppy. "You spoil everything for us. I wish we'd left you in Warsaw."

Jan, who had as usual acted from the highest of motives, began to protest. "Don't go for me, Ruth. I haven't stolen anything. The larder window was open all night, and I could have taken anything I wanted, but I didn't — you know I didn't!"

"Go on your knees and apologize," said Ruth.

He didn't go on his knees, but he did mutter that he was sorry. And the farmer, who had by now removed most of the traces of bomb damage from his neck and was almost ready to see the funny side of the situation, was gracious enough to take the apology in good part.

"Now, Mr. Interpreter," said the farmer to Edek, "perhaps you'll be good enough to explain your presence here."

Briefly Edek told him who they were, where they had come from, where they were going to, and why they had not (as they usually did) asked permission last night to sleep in the barn. They had arrived after dark and had not liked to disturb the household. "We'll willingly pay for our night's lodgings with a day's work," he finished.

"Of course," said the farmer. "And if I'm not satisfied with you, I'll hand you over to the Burgomaster."

"What's a burgomaster?" said Bronia, when Edek had interpreted (and from now on, he had to explain everything, for the farmer knew little Polish).

"A burgomaster, my dear, is a nasty bogey-man who plagues everybody beyond endurance. He'd be particularly interested in you. You're Poles, aren't you? Well, there's an order gone out from the Military Government that all Poles in the area are to be rounded up and sent back to Poland. It's the Burgomaster's job to see that the order is obeyed."

"We've just come from Poland. We're not going back again," said Ruth.

"We're going to Switzerland to find our father and mother," said Bronia.

"Nothing on earth would send me back to Poland," said Edek.

"Nor me," said Jan.

"That's what *you* think. But if the Military Government decides you must go back, back you go, my lad. And neither rotten turnips nor anything else will save you," said the farmer.

"Now come along and have a bite of breakfast."

There were window boxes on the sills of the farmhouse, gay with flowers. On the scrubbed table in the kitchen a breakfast of coffee and rolls for two had been laid.

"Emma!" called the farmer. "Four visitors for breakfast — four tattered bundles of mischief from Poland. Ruth, Edek, Jan, and Bronia. They've walked all the way specially to meet us. This is Frau Wolff, my wife. She speaks Polish. Learned it from two Poles who worked here during the war."

A plump and comfortable-looking lady shook hands with each of them in turn and, welcoming them to the table, went to fetch more breakfast. From now on, what with her knowledge of Polish and Edek's of German, the conversation ran quite smoothly.

"What's that mess on your collar, Kurt?" she asked when she came back.

"A present from Poland," said the farmer, winking at Jan, and when Edek translated, they all laughed so much that they nearly spilled the coffee.

"It was a clean shirt this morning," she complained.

"Then I shall ask Jan to wash it for me, just to show my appreciation."

"That's a wonderful idea," said Ruth.

"No doubt Jan would have thought of it himself, only I beat him to it," said the farmer, winking at Ruth.

"Jan has plenty of ideas, but not that sort," said Ruth.

"Eat all you can," said Frau Wolff, depositing a plate of rolls on the table. "There's plenty more when you've finished this lot."

Bronia's eyes were wide with astonishment. Never had she seen so much food.

"This is a farm, you know," Frau Wolff explained. "There is no shortage."

The family was content.

"You have made us so welcome," said Ruth, "I feel somehow as if you'd been expecting us."

"Oh, you get to expect anything in these parts," said the farmer, between gulps of coffee. "The woods are full of refugees like yourselves, you know. You're not by any means the first lot I've found in the barn. Last winter I found a whole family in the cowshed, curled round a cow to keep warm. Told me they'd walked all the way from the Ukraine. Didn't believe a word of it, of course. If you ask me, they'd just footed it from the next village — a stunt to get a free meal. I made 'em work for it, though. We've had dozens and dozens of refugees working here at one time or another. Got rid of them all now, thank the lord. Now the Military Government sends us nothing but German prisoners of war, and *they're* worse. The Government wants to turn us into an agricultural country. Holy onions, did you ever hear such nonsense! As if you could ever teach a mechanic how to milk a cow! He'd try it with a wrench if you didn't tell him how."

The farmer rambled on like this for some time, munching great mouthfuls of bread between whiles and washing it down with cascades of coffee. Edek was the only one who bothered to listen, and when at last the farmer came to a full stop he said, "I worked on a German farm during the war. But I hated every moment. The people weren't decent like you."

The farmer appeared to take this harmless observation as an insult. "You think I'm decent, do you? Just wait till I've wrung a day's work out of you — you'll think very differently then. We'll start right now, as soon as you're done eating."

"Let them rest today, Kurt," said his wife. "They're all of them worn out."

The farmer thumped the table with his fist. "I don't believe in treating people soft," he said. "Treat 'em rough, and they respect you. Give 'em the milk of kindness, and it'll turn sour. No, they'll start right now. Ruth and Jan shall come with me to the hayfield, and there'll be no lunch for them if they slack off. Bronia can feed the hens, and Edek —"

"Edek shall stay in the kitchen to help me," said his wife. "He looks as if a breeze would snuff him out. He shall stay and peel the potatoes for me — that is, if he'd care to." And the look she gave her husband made it quite clear that she intended to have her own way in this matter.

"Jan, you rascal, don't imagine I'll let you forget my shirt," said the farmer, thumping the table so fiercely that all the crockery jumped.

And, as far as Jan was concerned, the farmer had his way.

CHAPTER 20

THE BURGOMASTER

K URT WOLFF'S farm was high up in the Bavarian hills, not very far from the Czechoslovakian border. The hills were thickly wooded right to the top, and between them the River Falken came racing and twisting down on its way to join the Danube. A road passed through the field at the foot of the farm — northward toward Berlin, southward to the plains beyond the Danube. A few miles downstream was the village of Boding, where each day the Burgomaster received his unwelcome orders from the American troops stationed there. He was a tall, thin man in late middle age, a scientist and Social Democrat, who had lived in retirement from the rise of the Nazis in 1933 till the Americans fished him out some months back. He was shrewd and conscientious in a rather stupid way, but the antifraternization laws had soured him. He thought that Germans who were willing to cooperate with the Americans should be treated as friends, not as enemies. As go-between for his own people and the occupying power, he was answerable to both, and invariably received more kicks than praise.

In the eyes of the family he was the devil himself. His present instructions were to round up all Polish and Ukrainian refugees in the area and dispatch them home in the American lorries provided. Most of them (and there were a considerable number lurking in the hills and villages) were only too glad to be going home, but there were some who, like the family, had their reasons for not returning. It was up to them to keep clear of him, for orders were orders and must not be disobeyed. So the farmer had offered to keep the family with him till the scare was over. They were only too pleased to accept, for they had quickly found out that, however much thunder there might be in his words, there was little in his heart. And his wife cared for them as if they were her own family.

Jan, whom the farmer always referred to as the "exconvict," was particularly happy. He said that life on the farm was every bit as good as his week in prison. This he regarded as an achievement, and Ruth had quite failed to shake his pride in it. He made friends with an elderly and languishing mongrel dog named Ludwig. Until his arrival, it had lain dopily in the sun all day, resenting any attention shown to it. To anyone who did not know Jan, the vitality and devotion which he managed to coax out of this half-dead creature was astonishing. It followed him all over the farm wherever he happened to be working. He worked hard and with enjoyment. Nevertheless, like the others, when the lorries of cheering home-going refugees swept up the road each evening, he was careful to keep out of sight. He, too, was afraid of the shadow of the Burgomaster.

Once the Burgomaster paid a surprise visit, but the noise of his jeep rattling up the drive was warning enough, and they managed to reach the attic just in time. They lay there in the dust, all four of them, till he had gone. To their annoyance, the attic window was blocked up, and they failed to get a peep at him.

Later, when they were down in the parlor, Jan pointed to a man's photo on the mantelpiece and said, "Does the Burgomaster look like that?"

"Oh no," said Frau Wolff, "he's not as handsome or as young as that."

"Would he shoot us if he found us here?" said Bronia.

"He'd be more likely to shoot *me* for hiding you here," said the farmer. "But he's such a poor shot he'd probably hit *you* by mistake. Of course, our friend the exconvict is the one he ought to shoot."

"Let's talk about something more cheerful," said Ruth. She was admiring the smiling face of the young man in the photograph. She asked who it was.

"That's my elder son," said Frau Wolff, without looking up from her knitting. "Father took the photo on his last leave, before he went overseas."

"You never told us you had any children," said Edek.

"We haven't," said Frau Wolff. "Hans was killed in the desert at a place called Tobruk. Rudolf — he's in the other photo — standing at the back, in uniform — Rudolf died later, fighting to keep the Russians out of Warsaw."

"You mean he was in General Model's army?" said Edek.

"Yes."

"We might have seen him," said Jan, who was peering intently at the figure in the photo. "They all wore uniforms like that. They used to hide in the ruins and take pot shots at us if we dared to come out of our rabbit holes. We hated them."

"I liked them," said Bronia. "They used to give me sweets."

"That was the Russians. You've got the wrong army," said Jan.

"Some of the Germans were nice," said Ruth, "especially in the early days of the war."

Jan looked at Frau Wolff, quietly intent on her knitting; then at the farmer, whose eyes had a gleam of sadness he had not seen before; then back at the photo. That there could be any connection between these homely folk and the soldier in the photo was beyond his understanding.

After a moment he turned to the farmer and said, "You and I ought to be deadly enemies."

"The only deadly enemy you have," said the farmer, "is the Burgomaster, and even he has not given you much cause for complaint as yet."

"You wouldn't have hated Rudolf, Jan," said Frau Wolff.

"How do you know?"

"Because he loved Ludwig in the same way that you do. He trained him to be the best watchdog we ever had. He pined away when Rudolf was called up, but now that you've come he's almost as fit as he used to be. You're like Rudolf in other ways, too."

"Oh," said Jan.

"He was sent to Warsaw to kill us," said Ruth. "I don't suppose he wanted to very much. If he were here now, he would treat us as friends, as you do, Frau Wolff. It all seems so stupid and senseless."

"You'd like to be our mother, wouldn't you, Frau Wolff?" said Bronia.

"Yes, my dear, I would. I'd like to have you all. But you've got your own mother, and the most we can do for you is try to help you find her." She turned to Jan. "You have no mother, Jan. Would you like to stay here?"

"Yes, I would. Because of Ludwig. But I'd rather go with Ruth. Anyway, the sword wouldn't let me stay here, however much I wanted to."

"What sword?" said Frau Wolff.

Having mentioned the sword, there was nothing for it but to go and fetch it from his treasure box.

"It's beautifully made," said Frau Wolff. "Where did you get it?"

He told her how Joseph Balicki had given it to him long ago; how Ruth had discovered it; how it had been ever since a pledge that Joseph was still alive and waiting for them; how, when their spirits flagged, it gave them hope and inspired them to go on. Then he put it on the mantelpiece beside the photo of Rudolf, and a shaft of sunshine from the window caught it and made the silver blade sparkle.

Next day Edek and the "exconvict" were stooking hay together when a jeep swept past on the road, throwing up a cloud of dust behind it. It was traveling twice as fast as it should have been, and had just vanished behind a clump of trees when there was a loud explosion, a grinding of gears, a yell, then silence.

"Must have hit a tree," said Jan.

"It's a flat tire," said Edek. "Come on. We'd better go and help. Someone called out — he may be hurt."

"No. You don't know who it may be. Edek, come back!"

But Edek was halfway across the field already. He ran through the copse and found the car between two trees, at right angles to the road. The windscreen was cracked, and a middle-aged man was fumbling with one hand at the doorcatch, wiping blood from his forehead with the other.

"Flat tire," he said, as he stumbled out. "Flung me right off the road." He knelt down by the front wheel. "Cover's ripped right through."

"Are you all right?" said Edek in German.

"Yes, yes. Have you got a handkerchief? This one's getting rather messy."

"Afraid I haven't," said Edek.

"Never mind, I'll manage with this."

The cut was not deep, and after a minute or two the blood was flowing more slowly.

Together they checked the jeep for damage. Apart from the flat tire and cracks in the corner of the windscreen, where it had struck a branch, there was nothing else.

"Today of all days, when I'm in such a hurry!" the man exclaimed.

"I'll help you change the wheel," said Edek.

Anxious to help, Edek forgot to be suspicious and he set to work with the brace to unfasten the spare wheel, while the man, his handkerchief pressed to his forehead, stood by and watched. Out of the corner of his eye Edek stole a glance at him, and knew at once that it was the Burgomaster. The thought did not worry him unduly, for his German was sound enough to pass most tests.

"Working for Kurt Wolff?" the man asked.

"Yes. He takes on extra help at this time of year."

"I thought all his refugees had gone."

Edek started to cough. The effort to lift the spare wheel from its casing was too strenuous.

The man threw down his blood-soaked handkerchief and heaved off the wheel. "You take a rest," he said.

Just then Ludwig turned up, and that meant that Jan was somewhere around. Wagging his tail, he licked Edek's hand.

While the man was jacking up the damaged wheel, Edek felt something drop at his feet — an acorn. He looked up and saw Jan high up in the leafy branches, making frantic signs to him.

"Where do you come from?" the man asked, as he unscrewed the nuts.

"The north."

"Oh. I took you for a refugee. Can you give me a hand with the spare — I seem to have wrenched my arm a bit."

Edek tried, but the effort made him cough again.

"I'm sorry. I shouldn't have asked you. What about the lad up the tree — would he give a hand?"

Edek was taken aback. "Someone up in the tree?" he said lamely, then added, "It's my brother. Come down, Franz."

But Jan, who thought the man had not noticed him, was most reluctant to come down.

"Come down and lend a hand, Franz," Edek shouted, then explained to the man, "I'm afraid Franz is a bit deaf."

This time Jan came down.

"So you come down from the north, Franz?" said the man, in a loud voice. And when Jan did not reply, he added, "Seems to be dumb as well."

"Yes," said Edek, making a sign to Jan.

Jan took his cue, acting blank and stupid while he helped the man heave the spare wheel on. Edek thought he was overdoing it, with his vacant looks and gurgling noises, but the man did not seem to notice anything unusual.

The wheel was on and the man ready to drive off. Edek was congratulating himself on their success when suddenly Bronia arrived on the scene and spoke to them in Polish. Edek tried to cover it up by replying in German. He was surprised that the man still took no notice.

Switching the engine on, the man thanked the boys profusely for their help, backed the jeep on to the road and drove off.

"You're a couple of worm-eaten lunatics," said Jan feelingly.

"What did you want to climb into that tree for?" said Edek.

"To warn you it was the Burgomaster."

"I knew that — even a worm-eaten lunatic could tell that. Anyway, I think we got away with it."

"That's what *you* think," said Jan.

CHAPTER 21

ORDERS

THE farmer was at the kitchen sink washing the morning's grime from his face. His wife was always complaining that he left most of it on the towel instead of in the water. On this occasion he was running true to form, for his eyebrows were still white and foamy with soap when he reached out to dry himself. The towel wasn't there.

"Emma!" he shouted. "Will you never learn to put out a fresh towel when the soiled one goes to the wash? Emma!"

He heard heavy footsteps in the room, and in an unexpectedly brief time a towel was slipped into his hands.

"Thank you, my dear," he said. And when he'd wiped off all the soap and it was safe to open his eyes, he saw before him, not his wife, but the Burgomaster.

151

"It was over the back of the chair," said the Burgomaster. And he sat down on the edge of the kitchen table, which was his usual perch when he came on business.

"I envy you your farm, Kurt." It was one of the days when the Burgomaster was feeling sorry for himself. "It's so peaceful — cows grazing, cocks crowing, sowing and reaping, the eternal rhythm of the seasons. You're down to the things that really matter. You can have my job any day. All kicks and no thanks. The Americans curse me day and night, and when I pay a call on our own people I know they'd cut my throat if they could get away with it. I've come to requisition their houses, their furniture, their radios, their food, or — "

"Get to the point, Mr. Burgomaster. You want something out of me. What is it?"

"Another tiresome order — nothing to do with me, of course. All Polish and Ukrainian refugees are to be sent home, and tomorrow's the final date allowed."

"Oh, that's stale news. I lost the last of my refugees weeks ago, and you know it."

"You're hiding Polish children here," said the Burgomaster, and he told him about the previous day's adventure on the road.

"Well, and if I am?"

"They must go home like the rest."

"They don't want to. Their parents are in Switzerland, and they're going to find them."

The Burgomaster laughed. "I've heard that one before. Anyone in trouble at home always makes for the west — France or Switzerland. The Swiss are getting very choosy — too many nasty pieces have been getting through, political troublemakers, secret agents too. Even if we let these children go — and there's no chance of that — the Swiss wouldn't play. Not without definite proof that one parent was alive and already in the country."

"Emma!" the farmer called out. "Is Edek about the place?"

Frau Wolff answered from upstairs. "He's out in the yard."

"Will you tell him the Burgomaster would like to meet him?"

The farmer took the silver sword from the mantelpiece and showed it to the Burgomaster. "Here's proof that their tale isn't moonshine," he said, and he told him the story of the sword.

The Burgomaster laughed again. "Only a fool would accept that as proof," he said. "The mother's either dead by now or back in Poland, and there's not a chance in a thousand that the father got through Germany alive."

"I know he's alive," said Edek, who had just come in. "I know it in my heart." And he took the sword from the Burgomaster and put it back on the mantelpiece.

The Burgomaster shook hands with him. "Thank you, Edek, for what you did for me yesterday. You have a generous spirit. I wish I could treat you as generously. Your German is faultless, and your accent quite deceived me. Where did you learn our language?"

Edek told him of the months he had spent in Germany during the war.

"How you must hate us!" said the Burgomaster.

"I hate the Nazis who took Mother and Father away and blew up our home and destroyed our city. But all Germans are not like that."

"Were you in the fighting at Warsaw?"

"Yes," said Edek. "I was in the Boys' Rifle Brigade. I joined when I was twelve." And he thought of the night he had fired from his bedroom window when they took his mother away.

"Some weeks ago two of my villagers were shot by a Polish boy not much older than you. Like you, he had learned his job in the Boys' Rifle Brigade. He climbed through the bedroom

window and shot these people while they slept. He had nothing against them; I don't think he even knew who they were. You understand why we have to be careful. There have been other cases, too. Ever since the war ended the woods have been the hiding place of refugees who loot mercilessly and murder for revenge. Of course they are not all like that. But it is in everyone's interest that they should go home.

The Americans are inflexible on this point, and I don't blame them."

"Will he let us go, Edek?" said Ruth, who had come in with Bronia, Jan, and Ludwig.

"No," said Edek, and he told them what the Burgomaster had said.

"A lorry will come for you tomorrow at twelve midday," said the Burgomaster. "I shall expect you to be ready. Out of friendship I warn you not to try to escape. There is only the one road, as you know, and it's guarded by patrol posts. The woods are patrolled too, and the Americans may shoot at sight."

Ruth, who had followed the gist of this, began to plead with him in Polish. She told Edek to beg him to take their case direct to the Americans.

"Quite hopeless," said the Burgomaster wearily. "It has been tried many times, and with no success. The only thing they would consider is a pass from the Swiss authorities, and that is out of the question."

"In twenty-four hours, yes," said the farmer. "But it might be obtained if you would grant them longer."

"The time limit has been fixed, and not by me," said the Burgomaster curtly. "Good-by." He bowed stiffly and went.

Ludwig, who was no fonder of the Burgomaster than anybody else, was growling and barking, and Jan clung on to his collar. "Shall I let him go, Ruth? I'd love to see him bite a hole in the seat of the Burgomaster's trousers — and his shirt tail hanging out."

Ruth slipped her hand into Ludwig's collar. She did not let go till she heard the jeep's engine start up.

In a cloud of dust the jeep sped off down the farm track toward the main road, with Ludwig an inch or two behind. And the hills all round echoed his indignant barking.

CHAPTER 22

THE FARMER HITS
ON A PLAN

THE farmer did not normally milk the cows himself — that was left to others. But when he felt depressed or in need of a little reflection, he sometimes took his turn. To sit on a stool with his forehead pressed against a cow's flank and the milk splashing between his fingers into the pail — this, he found, was an attitude which inspired reflective thought.

All afternoon he had been wondering how to beat the Burgomaster and get the little family safely away. Telegrams to the International Tracing Service, to Berne, and to the Swiss consul in Munich, a hideout in a cave in the hills — these and other unfruitful ideas had flashed across his mind. Having by milking time found no solution, he took himself to the cowshed. And there, at the fifteenth splash into the pail, the idea sprang into being.

As soon as the milking was done, he assembled the family and took them up into the attic. Under a dusty heap of brown paper, broken cases, boys' skis, and some old boots, he found two long canvas bags. Their leather handles were green with mildew. It must have been years since anyone had touched them.

"Ruth and Jan can take this one, Edek can help me with the other," said the farmer. "Mind, they're heavier than they look. Bronia, you come down last and close the trap door behind us. Be careful not to fall down the ladder."

Wholly mystified, the family did as they were told.

In a pother of dust by no means to Frau Wolff's liking (she was rolling pastry), the bags were dumped on the kitchen floor. She made them take them into the yard.

So out they staggered with their burdens. A few stray hens flew clucking away. And the children clapped their black hands against their clothes.

"Gently, gently," said the farmer, as they fumbled clumsily with the fastenings.

Ruth's bag was the first to open. On top of musty lengths of stuff — was it canvas, was it rubber? — lay a bundle of sticks with metal clasps at the end. Whatever could it be?

Now the other bag was open, and the contents looked similar.

"Don't mix the two up," said the farmer. "I'll assemble the one while you all watch. You can do the other yourselves." And when asked for the umpteenth time what it was all about, all he would say was, "Ah!"

Out came the sticks first, and with the metal clasps the farmer joined them together — six sets of much the same length, which he fastened at the ends. The sticks grew into a skeleton. And before the farmer had started to give it flesh, Jan cried out, "A canoe!"

"It's a bit of a gamble," said the farmer, "but your only chance. Has any of you ever canoed before?"

"Yes," said Ruth and Edek both together.

"Father took us one summer in the Pieniny Mountains," said Ruth. "We hired two-seaters to take us downstream, then sent them back by train."

"One of these is a two-seater," said the farmer. "They belonged to my sons. Have you tried wild water?"

"The Dunajec wasn't particularly wild, except in one place where there were some rocks sticking out," said Edek.

"There are only two difficult patches on the Falken River," said the farmer, "the rapids ten kilometers below the village, and the part where the river joins the Danube. Keep to mid-stream and clear of the broken water, and you'll be all right." He did not tell them just how tricky the rapids were, and that it was a long time before he had allowed his boys to tackle them unaccompanied. Nor did he drop a hint of his other fear. The canoes were years old. Would they still hold the water out?

Working together, Edek and Jan assembled the second canoe according to the farmer's directions. After a time, soiled and battered but recognizable, two canoes lay stretched out on the ground.

"Of course we'll have to try them out," said the farmer, "and it's advisable to leave that till after dark."

"What about the paddles?" said Edek.

A second visit to the attic produced three double paddles, one of them snapped in two, another with a broken blade. The farmer saw to the carpentry, having packed the family off to a meal and bed. They must get a few hours' rest, for the plan would not work unless they were away in the small hours of the morning while it was still dark. There were many other things that could go wrong. Parts of the river were highly dangerous. Was any watch kept upon it where it ran past the village? Much luck and not a little skill would be needed for the venture to succeed. But it was their only chance.

It took the farmer till dark to repair the the paddles and the cracked floorboards. Of the four buoyancy balloons (one for each end), three were punctured and the fourth had perished. There was no time to get hold of new ones, so the three had to be patched and made do.

The moon had not yet risen when, with tractor and trailer, he carried the canoes down to the river to try them out. The larger one was all right, but the single-seater leaked in several places. The top skin of waterproof linen seemed sound enough. It was the underskin of rubberized cloth which needed attention. All he had to help him was some talc, and working by flashlight, he made the best job of it he could.

Soon after 3 A.M. four sleepy-eyed youngsters were bundled into the trailer and driven over the bumpy track down to the river. Frau Wolff sat with them.

"I found the waterproofs which go with the canoes and I've mended them for you," she told them. "Mind you fit them tightly round the splashboards, or you'll get swamped. And I've packed you up some food as well."

"Go easy with the food, dear," shouted the farmer, above the noisy splutter of the tractor. "We don't want to sink them."

Reaching the river, he shut off the engine. Under the dark trees they could see the river only dimly, but the gentle rushing sound of the water was music in their ears. "On, on to the Danube . . . on to Switzerland," it sang.

"Say good-by to Ludwig for me," said Jan. "I shall miss him dreadfully."

"Ludwig's in the wood somewhere. I heard him bark," said Bronia.

"Ludwig's asleep in his basket at home," said Frau Wolff.

"Listen, all of you," said the farmer. "Your safety depends on your not making any stupid mistakes. Edek and Jan — you'd better take the two-seater. We'll stow the luggage with you. Put on these waterproofs; the elastic grips round your faces and wrists and round the splashboard. They'll keep the water out of the canoe. Ruth and Bronia — you'll both have to fit into one waterproof as best you can. Keep the waistband tight round the splashboard."

When they were all aboard and the little luggage they had was safely stowed, he gave them final instructions. "It's only fifty kilometers to the Danube, so you've not far to go. Keep to mid-stream where you can — the river's fastest there. There's no need to paddle much, except in the broken water where there are rocks. For the rest, just keep the canoes headed straight, and the current will do all the work. If you get into difficulties, draw in to the side. The water's sluggish there and quite shallow. Remember: not a sound as you pass the village. There's no moon now and you shouldn't be seen. But if there's any firing, lie as flat as you can. Good-by and good luck to you!"

"God bless you, my dears," said Frau Wolff.

"We can never thank you enough for all you've done for us," said Ruth.

"I'll paint a picture of the farm with both of you in it, and I'll remember you forever," said Bronia.

The two boys waved their paddles.

The farmer gave each bow a gentle push. Ruth, tightly squeezed with Bronia inside the ashwood rim of the single-seater, drove hard in with her paddle and headed for mid-stream, with Edek and Jan close behind. Glancing back over her shoulder, she saw the two pale figures under the trees waving silently — silently and, she thought, rather sadly. The darkness quickly swallowed them.

"It's lovely and warm in here, like being in a nest," said Bronia. "I'm so glad I'm in your boat, Ruth. I bet the others are envious."

They were in the grip of the current now, floating gently and steadily downstream. Edek and Jan were a length behind. She could hear the splash of their paddles in the water and Jan's voice calling. Had something gone wrong?

She backed water till they drew alongside.

"Don't shout, Jan," she said.

"We're down at the bows. There's something very heavy inside, Ruth," said Jan.

"Pass the stuff back to me. There's room astern," said Edek.

Jan lifted the waist of his waterproof clear of the rim and reached underneath.

"Ow! It's wriggling — it's alive — and wet!" said Jan.

"Perhaps a fish has come up through the bottom," said Bronia, much alarmed.

But Jan had guessed already what was hiding

there. The wet thing was a nose. The stowaway was Ludwig. He thrust up eagerly for air, licking Jan's fingers and wriggling with delight at the success of his plans. As for Jan, even if this unexpected passenger meant shipwreck, he could not have been better pleased.

CHAPTER 23

DANGEROUS WATERS

THE current was swift. In the darkness, the great wooded hills swept by. For a moment the moon peeped from a cloud and turned the rippling surface of the stream to silver.

"Stay away, moon," Ruth muttered. "Don't come out again till we've passed the village."

Side by side, the two canoes sped on. On the left bank the line of the hills curved downward. Were those dim shapes houses? Had they reached the village?

Again the moon appeared. It had chosen quite the wrong moment, for this was indeed the village, with houses crowded about both banks and, on the left bank, suddenly an open space with lorries in it. They were so close together that they were almost touching, and there were several rows of them. These must be the lorries that were to take the Polish refugees back to Poland. With a tightening of fear in her throat, Ruth realized that if they were spotted now, they would be taken back too.

"Look out for the bridge," said Edek.

He and Jan shot ahead, aiming for the center of the three arches. Edging away from the square, Ruth paddled towards the right-hand arch.

Edek's canoe shot under the arch and disappeared into the shadows. Too far to the right, Ruth got caught in sluggish water. She drifted broadside on to the base of the arch.

The water was noisy, and Ruth did not hear the footsteps on the bridge. But she saw a man's shadow on the water, and it was moving. She paddled frantically to get free.

"The water's coming in. I can feel it damp under me," said Bronia.

A man shouted, and his shadow leaned far out over the water.

The canoe was still across the base of the arch, with the water thrusting against each end, threatening to break its back. She jabbed hard with the paddle and managed to ease it a little.

The man was right overhead, shouting and waving, but she could not understand what he was saying. In the distance a dog was barking.

A pair of legs dangled over the parapet and scraped against the stone — an American soldier.

With a last effort she thrust at the stonework, and the canoe broke free. But the soldier had clambered down and jumped into the water where it was shallow at the side. He caught at the paddle and clung on.

Ruth tugged, twisted, then let go of it, and the canoe swung sideways into the shadows under the arch. The soldier, not expecting her to let go, toppled over backward and fell with a splash into the river.

As the canoe shot out beyond the bridge, Ruth realized that she was at the mercy of the current. Bronia had no paddle and could not help.

Two or three shots from the bridge whizzed past her cheek, and she pushed Bronia's head down against the canvas. She peered ahead to see if she could see anything of the other canoe. Then the moon went behind a cloud, and the darkness hid her.

There were no more shots now, but she felt helpless as the current drove them wherever it chose. On and on they sped, the water foaming against the bows, spitting and bubbling against the canvas.

"I'm sitting in the river," said Bronia.

But Ruth took no notice. "Edek! Jan!" she shouted.

As they rounded a bend, they were thrust toward the right bank. The river was quieter here, and soon they felt the bottom of the canoe scrape over pebbles and slow them to a halt.

Ruth put her hand over the side and down into the water and tried to shove them off. But they were stuck. There was a pale light in the sky now, and the rim of the hills stood out dark against it. It was still too dark to see much, but she could make out rocks in the water, rounded like hippos' backs.

"We'll have to get out and push," she said.

They stepped into the water, which was little more than ankle-deep, and at once the canoe floated. With the painter in her hand and Bronia beside her, she drew it gently along till they came to a large V-shaped rock that seemed to project from the bank. She pulled the canoe high and dry on to a shoal of pebbles, then lifted Bronia on to the rock.

"We must wait here till daylight," she said.

And they sat there shivering and clinging to each other till the shadows brightened and they could see the whole sweep of the river, white and broken in the middle, rock-strewn and shallow at either side, with the wood-muffled hills hemming it in, and not a soul in sight. No sign of Edek and Jan. They could not have felt lonelier.

Then Bronia saw something which gave them hope. Down in the water, near the point of the V-shaped rock, was a stick that looked as if it might serve as a paddle. She climbed down to get it and found it was the very paddle they had lost. This was luck indeed.

They turned the canoe over and poured the water out. Then, with new confidence, they launched it again. Stepping aboard, they headed for mid-stream. And the current caught them and carried them on toward the rapids.

The river grew faster, and the bank flashed past. Soon they were in a kind of gorge, where the river squeezed past great boulders, some of them as high as houses. Some of the swells were over a foot high, and the spray dashed over the bow and stung their faces. The water roared here so that even the loudest shout could not be heard. Out to the left there were huge oily surges that looked as if they would pound you down into the depths if you got caught in them.

Bronia closed her eyes and clung to her sister's waist. Ruth was not as scared as she had expected to be. With a triumphant sense of exhilaration she flashed in with her paddle, heading always for the open stream, away from the white broken water where the rocks lay hidden. Now and then a boulder loomed up, and she knew that if they struck it they would be dashed to pieces. But a quick dip of the paddle at the right moment was enough to shoot them safely past.

In no time the river broadened, the boulders eased, and the banks were wooded again. The terrors of the rapids were over. Ruth hoped that Edek and Jan, whose two-seater was much less easy to maneuver, had been as successful as they had.

There seemed no need for the paddle now, for the water was clear of rocks and the current smooth and swift. They could lie back and let the canoe take care of itself.

Bronia closed her eyes and fell asleep. Ruth lay back and watched the blue sky overhead and the climbing sun. It was to be another scorching day, and she too became sleepy and dozed.

A grating, tearing sound brought her to her senses, and she woke to find herself thigh-deep in water. The canoe had grounded on a shoal and a sharp stone had ripped the canvas underneath. She looked about her. The river was very broad here, and they were near the right bank, where it was shallow and easy to wade ashore. So they stepped out and scraped the waterlogged craft over the pebbles to the bank and hauled it ashore.

"The tear's too long to mend," said Ruth. "We shall have to leave the canoe and walk. It can't be far to the Danube now."

They found a path which threaded its way through the trees on the bank, and they followed it to the last big bend before the river joined the Danube at Falkenburg. There were no woods here, only green fields, a dusty country road, and a gently sloping bank that reached far out into the river.

Ruth made for the bank, for she thought it would give her a good view of the river in both directions and some chance of seeing Edek and Jan. Except for a couple of unfinished haystacks, the bank was deserted. She did not know that two sentries had posted themselves here for most of the morning, on the lookout for their canoe. Weary with waiting, they had climbed to the top of one of the haystacks and taken it in turns to go to sleep.

The first she knew of their presence was when a half-eaten apple struck her on the shoulder. Then there was a bark, and Ludwig was licking her ankles.

"Where have you been all this time? We thought you must have come to grief in the rapids," said Jan, who was standing on top of the stack. He gave the sleeping Edek a shove, and the boy landed, with hay sticking out of his hair and his shirt, right at Bronia's feet. It was a merry meeting.

"We came to grief too," said Edek, "same way as you did, but we traveled farther before we went aground."

Not a hundred yards away a convoy of American lorries swept up the road in a pother of dust. They were crammed with refugees, most of them Poles and all grimly silent. But the children were so busy talking and laughing over their experiences that they did not even notice.

CHAPTER 24

MISSING

THEY walked into Falkenburg, crossed the Danube, then got a lorry lift for some miles along the road to Switzerland. After this, more walking.

Three days later, tired and joyful, they camped by the roadside.

"Only eighty more miles to Lake Constance," said Ruth gaily, as she looked for a patch of rough, dry grass for Bronia to lie in.

"Is Lake Constance in Switzerland?" said Bronia sleepily.

"Switzerland is on the far shore of the lake," said Ruth. "Lie down here, Bronia. The grass is nice and thick."

"Will Mother be waiting for us on the shore?" said Bronia.

"Perhaps she will," said Ruth. And in the dim

light nobody noticed that her eyes were wet
with tears.

Jan's treasure box was one of the few things
which they had salvaged from the wrecked
canoes. He had been too busy to think about it,
but tonight he decided to open it, to make sure
that all his treasures were safe. With Ludwig's
nose in his lap, he took the lid off and counted
them one by one. Suddenly he leapt to his feet.

"The sword's missing!" he said. "Someone's
stolen it!"

"Nobody would do that," said Ruth. "Let me
have a look."

She checked through the box, but the sword
wasn't there. Thinking carefully back to the last
time she had seen it, she said, "You showed it
to Mr. and Mrs. Wolff, Jan, and put it on the
mantelpiece beside Rudolf's photo. Did you
leave it there?"

For a moment Jan stopped his raging, then
grunted, "Yes," and ran off to the roadside.

Ruth said no more. Bronia lay curled in the
grass with a blanket over her, already half
asleep. Ruth gave her attention to Edek. Since
the river adventure he had been coughing more
than ever, and had complained more than once
that the pain in his chest was getting worse.

She was shocked to see how ill and haggard he looked. In her knapsack she had a jersey that Mrs. Wolff had given her. She made him put it on and lie down in his blanket.

Soon he stopped coughing and lay still. "Where's Jan gone?" he asked.

Ruth looked up. It was almost dark now, and Jan was nowhere to be seen. Nor was Ludwig. She stood up and called him. From way up the road a voice called back, "I'm going back for the sword."

"The silly little idiot," Ruth exploded, and she ran off after him. A few minutes later she brought him back. She told him off roundly, pointing out that the Wolff's were honest folk and would look after the sword until it was sent for.

Sullen, resentful, plunged in gloom, he said nothing at first. But when Ruth lay down to sleep, he muttered, "I'm going back all the same."

"Light a fire for us, Jan," said Ruth. "Edek's not well, and it will help him to sleep." It was a warm night and they did not need a fire. But she felt sure that Jan would not leave them once he put his mind to something practical. Nevertheless, when the fire was burning and the other three were sleeping, she forced herself to keep awake just in case.

At midnight the fire had died down to a red glow. She was still awake. Out of the darkness and the stillness a voice spoke, or rather gasped, her name.

"Edek! I thought you were asleep," she said.

"I can't sleep. The pain's too bad," said Edek. "I can't — go on — any farther."

"You'll feel better in the morning," said Ruth.

"Can't walk any more," said Edek.

"We'll get a lift. It's only eighty miles."

"There's no traffic going that way," said Edek.

She talked to him quietly for a while and, after another bout of coughing, he dropped off to sleep. But anxiety for him kept her awake. A change had come over him during the last twenty-four hours. If they did not reach Switzerland soon, he might not live.

The hours crept on, and still she did not sleep. Once more out of the stillness a voice called her name. This time it was Jan.

"Ruth, may I have Edek's shoes when he dies?" he said.

"He's not going to die," said Ruth, forcing herself to speak calmly.

"He will if I don't have my sword," said Jan.

"And we'll never find your father, either. He gave me the sword, and it's our guide and life-line. We can't do without it."

He spoke with such certainty that she almost believed him. It was true that, while they had the sword, fortune had been kind to them. And now Edek was more gravely ill than he had ever been. But all she said was, "Go to sleep, Jan. Everything will be all right."

Jan did not go to sleep; it was Ruth who slept. There came a time toward dawn when she could not keep her eyes open any longer.

The fire was cold and the sun peering over the rim of the hills when she woke. Jan and Ludwig had gone. A crumpled blanket and a half-moon of flattened grass showed where they had lain.

Her first thought was to run after Jan. Then a glance at the two sleepers reminded her that she had other responsibilities more pressing. Gently she touched Edek's hand. It had hardly any warmth in it. His face was frighteningly pale. Giving way to panic, she leaned over to listen for his breathing. Yes, he was breathing. Thank God for that. But he did not look as if he would be able to get up, let alone walk.

The road was empty, and there was nobody in sight. Her strong faith seemed to desert her and she felt more dreadfully alone than ever. Was it true what Jan had said about the sword?

With a fierce effort of will, she took herself in hand and began to prepare breakfast. There was still food in the knapsack left over from what Mrs. Wolff had given her.

Bronia was the first to wake, and she ate hungrily. She did not seem at all worried to find Jan and Ludwig gone. "Jan can look after himself," she said cheerfully.

"He forgets that we may need him to look after us," said Ruth.

The sun stealing over his drawn face woke Edek. He was too dazed to notice that Jan and Ludwig were missing. Ruth could not persuade him to eat anything.

"What's wrong with Edek? His eyes are all glassy," said Bronia.

"I expect it's the heat," said Ruth, and Bronia was satisfied with the answer. Though it was still early, the sun was already hot. Yet another scorching day was in store for them.

Ruth had almost to lift Edek to his feet. When she let go of him, he fell over. With Bronia's help she got him up again, and with their arms round him they staggered along to the roadside. Edek seemed just sensible enough to understand that he was expected to walk, and after a few paces he managed fairly well with just Ruth to steady him. But he looked as if he were sleepwalking, and it was only a matter of time before he must collapse.

"Shall we have a ride today?" said Bronia.

"Of course we shall," said Ruth.

"The driver said yesterday that there was no traffic on this road going to Switzerland," said Bronia.

"He was wrong," said Ruth. "Look — there's something coming now."

But it was only a laborer on a bicycle, who hardly gave them a glance as he passed by.

"I should have asked him for help," thought Ruth when, after an hour of painful walking, nobody else had appeared.

Then Edek collapsed. There were beads of sweat on his brow, and he kept muttering, "I can't go on. I can't go on." Ruth dragged him into the shade and told Bronia to stay by the roadside and stop the first person that passed.

A woman in slacks came by, pushing a barrow. She seemed to be looking for firewood. Ruth made her understand that they wanted help, but she shrugged her shoulders and made off. A little later a lorry with a tarpaulin roof stretched over a frame came along. At Bronia's signal, it braked to a halt. She called to the driver in Polish. He was an American G.I. His face lit up when he heard her speak, and to her astonishment he answered her in her own language.

He stepped down from the lorry, lighting a cigarette as he did so.

"Have you come from Poland too?" said Bronia, forgetting her errand for the moment.

"Not exactly. My parents were Polish, but I'm from the States myself," said the man. "We went there before the war. Joe Wolski's my name — just call me Joe. It's good to hear a Polish voice again." He bent down and took her hands in his. "Now, lady. What's your trouble?"

CHAPTER 25

JOE WOLSKI

THEY squashed into the front seat of the truck beside Joe Wolski, and off they rattled on the road to Switzerland.

"You'll be telling me next that you've come all the way from Warsaw," said Joe.

"So we have," said Bronia.

"Gee, that's some way," said Joe. "I guess the city's changed since I was there before the war. I was only six when Ma and Pa took me to the States to settle. I like it a lot over there now, and I can't say I'm sorry we made the move. How's the kid doing?"

The "kid," Edek, was sitting by the door where the fresh air from the open window had already revived him.

"Would he like a cigarette?" said Joe.

Edek shook his head.

"What about you, lady?"

Ruth refused as well, and she watched Joe take both hands off the steering wheel to light a cigarette for himself — and suddenly jab in an elbow to correct a swerve. After her almost sleepless night, she was too tired to do anything but lie back with her head against the top of the seat. In spite of their good luck in securing a lift, she could not shake off her anxiety for Edek.

The countryside swept by — trees and hills and villages — and after a while Ruth roused herself from her sadness and asked Joe where he was taking them.

"You leave that to me, lady," he said. "You've plenty on your mind, and you've told me where you want to go."

"But we hardly know who you are or what you're doing."

"I'm the Occupation," he said. "The army taught me French so I could go to Paris, then posted me to Germany because I can't speak German. I'm here to fire folks with the spirit of occupation, to tell them they've all grown up the wrong way. But what's the use? They're so sick and tired, they just stare at you. It's not often you get a chance to help someone . . . Gee, that was a close shave!"

Joe had been trying to light another cigarette, and the lorry had swerved across the road, skidded, and nearly knocked down a tree. He righted her just in time, blew the tree a kiss, and drove on.

"What was that noise?" said Bronia. "I thought I heard a yelp. You haven't run over —"

"No, no," said Joe. "Just the tires complaining, I expect. You get used to it. Now talking about growing up wrong, that tree's a case in point. Only a muttonhead would have let it grow there."

"Nonsense," said Ruth. "It's well off the road. Be sensible and let me hold the wheel while you light up."

After a while Bronia asked, "What's in the back of the truck, Joe?"

"Never you mind," said Joe.

"Could I sit in the back?" said Bronia.

"You wouldn't like it," said Joe. "There's a couple of bears and a hyena in there."

"Jan would love that," said Bronia.

"Who's Jan? Is he your boy friend?" said Joe.

Bronia giggled and told him he was a friend who had run away.

"Oh," said Joe, and a suspicion of a smile stole across his face. "Why did he run away?"

Bronia told him all about it, and when she had finished Joe said, "I once knew a kid who ran away like Jan. I had gone to sleep in the back

of my truck — alone, mark you — and when I
woke in the morning, there he was, stretched
out beside me. Must have climbed in over the
tailboard during the night. I shook him awake
and asked what the heck he was doing. Said he
was going north, and if I was going that way
would I take him to . . . I forget the name of
the village. Some place north of the Danube.
Now I *was* going north as it happened, but when
I heard his business I changed my mind. I told
him he ought to have known better than to
desert his folks. He kicked and stormed at me
as if he was crazy and called me all the names
that aren't in the dictionary. Know what to do
with a fella like that? You truss him up and
leave him to cool off in the back of the truck till
he knows better. And that's just what I did."

There was a question already on Bronia's lips,
when she heard a bark from behind her.

"That must be the hyena," said Joe. "Like to
take a look?"

He stopped the truck by the side of the road,
and Ruth and Bronia followed him out and
round the back. He hoisted them up into the
hyena's cage. There on the floor in front of a
pile of crates was Ludwig, barking and wagging
his tail, and Jan beside him, with a handkerchief
over his mouth and his wrists and ankles bound.

Joe undid his bonds and said with a broad grin, "How are you feeling, kid?"

Jan's answer was to kick out at Joe and spit at him like a catherine wheel, while the elderly and good-natured Ludwig crouched in a corner growling, but not quite knowing what to make of it all.

"It was true what I told you about a couple of bears and a hyena," said Joe. "Here they are, all rolled into one."

Ruth begged Jan to stop kicking, but he took no notice.

"Does this make you feel better?" said Joe, and he threw him a slab of chocolate.

Jan threw it back again.

"Nothing for it but to tie up the parcel again," said Joe, and as Jan would not listen to Ruth's reasoning he had to carry out the threat. He managed with some difficulty to tie Jan to the tailboard in such a way that he could not throw himself out, but left his ankles unbound and his mouth free.

And off they went. The lorry made quite a lot of noise on the bumpy road, but not half as much as Jan made. In this manner they journeyed the sixty odd miles to Lake Constance, right to the gate of the Red Cross camp where Joe had planned to take them. It was a collection of tents and Nissen huts between Überlingen and Meersburg, within a stone's throw of the lake. The hills round about were thickly wooded, and trees crowded the shore. Through a gap in the trees, across the water could be seen the green hills of Switzerland and behind them, in a haze of sunshine, the majestic Alps.

Ruth gasped. The mountains were more beautiful than anything she had ever imagined. They looked so near that she could almost lean over and touch them.

The motion of the truck had rocked Edek to sleep, and he only stirred when Ruth and Bronia shouted and clapped for joy.

"Please can you let Jan out?" said Ruth. "He'll feel quite different if you show him the mountains of Switzerland."

Joe untied him. Jan was quiet and sober, for he had kicked and shouted till he had no more kick or shout in him. He accepted some chocolate, and when Joe put an arm round his shoulders and pointed to the mountains they had come so far to see he burst into tears.

CHAPTER 26

NEWS AT LAST

JOE did not find it easy to persuade the camp to take in the family. It was not at the moment overcrowded — in fact, a whole party of refugees had recently been sent back to their countries — but it was in a muddle. The decision to make this corner of south Germany part of the French Zone had only been taken in the middle of June. Now it was August, and the Americans were beginning to hand over to the French. The muddle helped Joe to get his way. It also helped Ruth to get hers. The camp doctor wanted to separate the family, with Edek in the Nissen hut which served for a hospital and the rest in E block at the other end of the camp. Ruth refused to leave him. Finally she was allowed one of the tents outside the hospital block within call of Edek's bed, and here under canvas the three of them made their home.

There was one matter in which the camp superintendent refused to budge. He would not allow the family to cross over into Switzerland. The Swiss authorities could take no more refugees unless there were relatives in the country willing to be responsible for them. Besides this, they needed some definite proof of identity before any arrangements could be started upon.

Ruth thought that the sword might help to prove who they were, and she wrote at once to the farmer for this. As for relatives in Switzerland, she did not even know if her father had ever arrived there. Nor could she remember her grandparents' address in Basel. She had no idea if they were still alive.

She was feeling sad and disheartened when she said good-by to Joe. They had come so far, and now that their goal was within sight it seemed harder than ever to reach. She thanked him from the bottom of her heart for all his kindness.

"Don't call me kind," said Joe. "Everywhere's a mess, wherever you look. I want to help clean it up. I want to show folks that you can't see all of life from a hole in a blitzed cellar. There's more to it than ruins and rubble. Sometimes things work out right and sometimes they don't."

As he shook Ruth's hand, he added, "This time they're going to work out right."

One by one the hot, stifling days dragged by. There was thunder in the air, but the black clouds held back their rain. They seemed to be saving it up for some grand and terrible occasion. Had it not been for Edek, who was too ill to be out of bed for more than a few hours each day, the others would have borrowed a small boat and risked the crossing. But Edek's illness kept them back — that and the hope that the I.T.S. (International Tracing Service) would soon answer the superintendent's letter. He had lost no time in sending them all the information that Ruth had given him. His inquiries in Basel for the grandparents had yielded no results. What was more surprising was that Ruth received no reply from Herr Wolff about the sword.

The I.T.S. occupied a huge barracks, once used by Nazi Storm Troopers, at Arolsen in the American Zone. In those early days of so-called peace, the child-search branch had hardly got going and was able to deal with inquiries quite quickly. But the index of missing children was growing all the time, as each day brought more and more inquiries. "Is my child dead?" "Our home was bombed while I was serving in Africa and I believe my younger daughter survived, but I have failed to trace her . . ." "My two sons were taken from me in Auschwitz in 1942 and adopted by a German family in Nuremberg. Can you, etc. etc. . . ." Inquiries like these arrived by every post.

One day, late in the month, the superintendent called Ruth to his office. Was it good news or bad? His face was as grave as usual and betrayed nothing. He spoke slowly. "That sword you told me about, Ruth. Would you describe it to me, please?"

She did so in great detail, even mentioning a tiny piece on the hilt which was slightly bent. As she described it and launched once again into the story of its adventures, a smile spread over his face.

"Ruth, you're the luckiest girl in Europe," he said, and he unrolled a small brown-paper parcel on his desk. Out of it tumbled two crumpled letters — and the sword. One letter was from Herr Wolff and the other from her father. Both were addressed, not to her, but to the headquarters of the I.T.S. Herr Wolff's letter contained as much of the story of the family as he had managed to piece together, as well as details of their plans for getting to Switzerland. He had found the sword the very day they

left and had sent it off at once to the I.T.S.
with the letter. Ruth's letter to him, written
from the camp, had evidently gone astray, for
she had no reply to it till weeks later. The other
letter, from her father, Joseph Balicki, bore a
January date. In it he described the children
and their circumstances up to the time when he
had last seen them. He also referred to his
escape from Zakyna, his unsuccessful attempt
to find his family, the meeting with Jan and how
he had given him the sword, and his long journey to Switzerland. And now the miracle had
worked!

Ruth was so overcome that all she could do
was bury her face in her hands. She hardly
heard what the superintendent was saying.

"I received this information two days ago,
but I didn't want to tell you till I had checked
it all. You see, your father's letter is months old,
and I had to get in touch with him. He's living
in Appenzell, just the other side of the lake.
Here's his reply to me."

He handed Ruth a telegram, but she was still
too dazed to take in all that he had said, and he
had to repeat most of it again. Brushing away
her tears, she read the message: "Will collect
children on 23rd at Meersburg by the afternoon boat. All arrangements about permits in

hand this end. Please wire answer. Will ring Ruth tonight if possible."

"I wish all our cases could end as happily as yours," said the superintendent.

But Ruth was already out of the room and running to her family to tell them the great tidings.

Five minutes later the Red Cross nurse on duty in E block heard a fearful row. Rushing into the last Nissen hut, she found three children and an elderly dog dancing up and down on Edek's bed. When she protested, they threw all his pillows at her. So she fetched a broom and chased the three of them down to the lake. Then she returned, angry and out of breath, to pick up the pillows and see if the patient had died of shock. But the patient had sneaked out of bed and, by a roundabout way, joined the others on the shore. For him, the news was more of a tonic than all the medicine and all the rest and care in the world.

Is that the end of the story?

The family, as they laughed and danced for joy on the shore, thought it was. They did not know that what was in some ways their most dangerous ordeal still lay ahead.

CHAPTER 27

THE STORM

Iᴛ was the morning of the twenty-third. Joseph Balicki had tried to speak to Ruth on the phone, as he had promised, but the line had been so bad that she did not recognize his voice and could hardly hear a word. He seemed to be trying to tell her something of importance, but after several unsuccessful attempts the line went dead, and that was the end of that. What was it he was trying to tell her? How she longed to see him again!

The Swiss boat that was to take them over the water was not due for some hours yet. But the family were too impatient to wait. They were down by lakeside, eager to catch a glimpse of her when she steamed past the distant Swiss shore. They looked very stiff in their best clothes. Edek was wearing one of Rudolf Wolff's suits, and Ruth a summer dress of his mother's. Jan was wearing a blue shirt,

and Bronia a cotton dress too small for her —
both had been given to them in camp. Their
faces, bronzed by the sun and dirtied by weeks
of dusty wandering, were unusually clean.
They had made valiant efforts to untangle hair
that hardly knew what brushes and combs
were for. Jan's hair had been so knotted that
he found a comb useless and had to resort to
a pair of scissors instead.

They were so excited that they did not
notice how heavy the air was and how dark
the clouds. Ludwig was unhappy and kept
whimpering, but none of them — not even Jan —
seemed to notice.

"Let's go on past that headland over there,"
said Jan. "We'll get a much better view of the
lake."

"It means we'll have to cross this stream,"
said Ruth.

"It's only a trickle," said Jan.

And that was true, for during that rainless
summer the stream that wound down the
wooded hills to the shore was far emptier than
usual. They could cross it easily by jumping
from boulder to boulder. Even Bronia need
not get her feet wet.

"I think I'll stay on this side," said Edek,
who was out of breath.

"Good idea," said Ruth. "Sit down on that

rock till we come back. I promise we shan't be long."

Nevertheless, when the three of them were across the stream, she felt suddenly uneasy without Edek. It seemed safe enough, but was it wise to leave him? After a moment's hesitation she called back to him, "Edek! There's a boat pulled up on the shore behind you, and it's half-decked in front."

"Well, what about it?" said Edek.

"You can shelter inside if it rains," said Ruth.

It was the first time that anyone had mentioned rain. Soon, as the three of them scampered along the shore towards the headland that Jan had pointed out, the first drops began to fall. Ruth looked back over her shoulder. She waved Edek toward the boat and saw him, with a laugh and a grimace, obey her.

"Is that the headland?" panted Bronia, as her short legs padded along beside her sister. "Shall we really see Father's ship coming?"

"Yes," said Ruth.

But if she had looked up she would have seen that the far side of the lake was hidden. In the gathering rain, even the headland they were making for was hazy.

Suddenly there was a great clap of thunder.

It rolled and echoed far away into the distant Swiss mountains. Lightning streaked through the black clouds, flickered along the wooded hills. The thunder and lightning were the heralds of what came to be known as the freak storm of 1945. Those who were caught in it were to remember it with horror all their lives. It was the climax of weeks of oppressive heat in which no rain had fallen.

Suddenly, in one huge downpour, the sky shed its burden of rain. It lashed the lake and beat upon their bare heads, and soaked them to the skin. In great blinding sheets it fell, so that they could not see where they were. Their ankles were deep in water. Had they stumbled into the lake, or was the shore flooding?

Ruth felt for Bronia's hand and clung to it. She felt for Jan's too, but he was trying to grip Ludwig's collar and calm him. She caught hold of his shirt, but he broke roughly away.

"We must go back to Edek," she said.

This was easier said than done. Her head was numb with the force of the rain, her eyes half closed. She bumped into a fallen tree, then, feeling her way with her one free hand, groped along the shore. It was some time before she realized that she was going in the wrong direction. Back again, slowly, with head bowed and feet floundering in mud and water and swirling pebbles.

In the hope that the rain would ease off, they sheltered under a small cliff, till the muddy overhang broke off and almost smothered them. She was running now, pulling the yelling Bronia and shouting to Jan to keep close.

They came to a place they did not recognize. A river had burst through the shore and was hurling itself into the lake.

"We'll never get across. Oh, Edek! Edek!" Ruth cried.

And they stood there with Bronia, watching helplessly as the current swept all kinds of things headlong into the lake: old oil cans, tires, planks, a wooden seat, part of a landing stage, whole trees. A canoe went by, bottom upwards. A dead sheep. A bough with a cat standing on it, its back arched in terror.

Suddenly she realized that the rain was easing and that she could see across to the other side. A sudden pang of anxiety struck her. This raging river was the little trickle of a stream they had crossed so effortlessly an hour ago. Edek must be on the other side.

But Edek was not there. Nor was the boat

which she had told him to shelter in if it rained.
Trees were standing in water; there seemed to
be hardly any shore at all, and the water was
all round them, up to their knees and rising
higher.

With an effort, she pulled Bronia clear, and
they flopped down on to some muddy ground
that the water had not yet reached.

"Where's Jan gone?" panted Bronia.

"I don't care where he's gone," said Ruth
bitterly. "I told him to stay with us, but he
went after Ludwig. Oh, Edek! Edek!" Brushing the wet hair from her eyes, she peered out
into the lake. If he had stayed in the boat, he
must have been washed out with it. In all the
flotsam and jetsam tossed about on the mud-
stained waves, she could see no sign of the boat.

"Jan's on the cliff behind," said Bronia.

Ruth turned. It was hardly a cliff, little more
than a bump of ground clear of the water.

"Can you see him from up there, Jan?" Ruth
called.

"He wriggled out of my arms and got away,"
Jan cried, and he was looking inland.

"I mean Edek — can you see his boat?"

But Jan didn't answer. He was thinking of
Ludwig.

Ruth ran up to him. She wanted to shake

him to pieces for being so selfish. But Bronia was calling.

"I think I can see Edek's boat out in the middle of the lake — it's miles away!"

Again Ruth swept the hair from her eyes. The boat was hardly more than a dark smear on the waves, but her instinct told her that it was Edek's and that he was in it. The fear that she felt now was greater than any fear she had ever known before. The boat vanished, and she sank down with her head in her hands.

And all the while the rain poured down and the ever-widening river carried with it more trees, more animals, dead and alive, more shore junk, far out into the lake. It brought with it a rowing boat too. Bronia was the first to see it.

At once Ruth jumped up and waded out for it. It was quite close to the bank, bumping along sluggishly, for it seemed half full of water. Nevertheless, when she caught hold of the side, it almost carried her away. It would have done so if Jan had not waded in to help.

"Go away and look for your dog," said Ruth bitterly. "You don't care about Edek. Go away — I hate you."

But Jan clung on. Together they dragged the boat clear of the current and on to the mud. They managed to tip out some of the water.

They found an oar jammed under the seats. In the locker at the stern were some rope and a baler. There were no rowlocks. They worked to make her as shipshape as they could. Ruth knew what she wanted to do now, but she did not speak of it. Instead she lashed Jan with her tongue.

"You never have cared about us. All you ever think about is your blessed animals. Look — there's Ludwig up there by the road. Run after him, and don't come back. Bronia and I can save Edek without you."

The two girls jumped into the boat. It needed

no pushing, for the water was already round it.

Jan was still gazing up the road at Ludwig. The dog was running round and round in circles, crazy with fear, half blinded by the rain — now making a sudden bolt inland. It was a bitter moment for Jan. More than anything in the world he wanted to go after Ludwig. But Ruth's words had hurt him. They had stirred something deep down in his heart, and he hesitated. With a great effort of will, he shed Ludwig from his mind and turned to his friends. In Ruth's face he saw what he had hardly noticed before, though they had long been there: courage, self-sacrifice, and greatness of heart. He hesitated no longer. He had lost Ludwig, but he had not lost Ruth. And the treasure box was still safe under his arm.

He threw the box into the boat, jumped in, and seized the oar. Sliding the oar over the stern, he shoved the boat into the current.

In that moment of decision Jan began to grow up.

And the boat was caught up in the swirl of the water and thrust far out into the lake, toward the heart of the storm.

CHAPTER 28

THE MEETING

IT was dark when Ruth opened her eyes. She was being lifted up.

A man's voice said, "It's a girl — thin as a string of seaweed and wringing wet. How you feeling, eh? We nearly ran you down in the dark."

He spoke in a strange language which Ruth did not understand. She tried to speak, but no words came.

"She's worrying about something," said the man.

"Better take her below and get some dry clothes on her," said someone else.

Her mind drifted to a blank.

When she woke again, she was lying in a bunk. There was a light above her, dry blankets round her, and a flicker of warmth in her limbs.

"Where am I?" she said.

Strange faces peered down at her from the sky. There was a cup at her lips.

"Feed her slowly," a man was saying. "Don't give her too much, or she'll be sick."

The cup came back again, and biscuits too. She sat up.

"Edek! Bronia! Jan!" she cried.

"Polish names," said a woman's voice. "I said she was Polish. Anyone talk Polish here?"

"Tell her about the others," a man said.

"Don't know the language."

There was a general cry of, "Anyone talk Polish?" and Ruth, frightened by the unfamiliar faces, cried out again, "Edek! Bronia! Jan!"

And suddenly from the back of the crowd came the echo, "Edek! Bronia! Jan!" in a deep voice. Dazed and bewildered though she was, she knew it for her father's voice. Now she was gathered in his arms, smothered with his kisses. She tried to speak, to listen to what he was saying. But her head was throbbing, and she was too tired to keep her eyes open.

When she woke again, her father's face was close to hers.

"You've been asleep a long time," he said.

"Try to stay awake, and I'll show you what you want to see."

The blankets pressed round her, and she felt herself being lifted from the bunk.

"Look down there," said Joseph.

She saw, in a nest of blankets, Bronia's sleeping head. There was a flush of color on the child's cheeks, and she was snoring.

"Nothing much wrong with her," said Joseph, and he carried Ruth to the next bunk.

She looked again and saw Edek's face. It was very white, and he was lying still and as straight as a post.

"Is he breathing?" she asked.

"Yes, he's breathing," said Joseph, "but only just." And he carried her quickly away and showed her Jan.

He was sitting on his blankets, dangling his legs over the edge of the bunk. There was a glint of mischief in his eyes.

"They're a feeble lot, the Balickis," he said. "They would all have drowned if it hadn't been for me. Ruth, you're crazy. Fancy going for a sail in weather like this — and thinking you could manage without me! You use an oar like a soupspoon, and when a little water comes in the boat you faint. I had to find Edek's boat and steer ours to it. I shouted to him to help, but he'd fainted too. The water was nearly up to his neck. So I pulled him over the side into our boat — two seconds before his turned over and sank."

Joseph patted his cheek affectionately. "Eat up your bread and cheese and stop boasting," he said. "If you say any more, you'll burst."

Ruth reached out her arms to Jan and gave him a hug. "You ought to be made an admiral at once," she said. "Thank God they're safe, all three of them." And then she flung her arms round her father's neck.

"You've got your numbers wrong. I haven't finished yet. Hey, don't strangle me!" he said. And he carried her out of the cabin.

"There *are* only three," said Ruth. "What do you mean?"

"The last and the best surprise," said Joseph, opening another door. "I tried to tell you over the phone, but I couldn't make myself heard."

The cabin was small, and there was only one person in it. She had been waiting for the door to open. Her eyes were wide with expectation, her arms stretched out in welcome.

"Mother!" said Ruth, and with a happiness that no words can describe she slipped from her father's arms into those other arms, so eager

to receive her. It seemed like a hundred years
since she had last seen her mother — on that
sad and brutal occasion when the Nazi Storm
Troopers had dragged her down the steps of
their Warsaw home. She had been in a con-
centration camp until, after months of patient
searching, Joseph had traced her through the
Red Cross. But that is another story. Four years
of suffering had turned her hair quite white,
and there were deep lines in her face. But
Ruth's heart was so full that she saw only the
joy and happiness there. And she thought of
the Daniel story, which she had so often told
to her schoolchildren. Now for her, as for Daniel, deliverance had come at last.

"Mother was sitting beside you all the time
you were asleep," said Joseph. "She went away
when you woke up. We didn't want to give
you too many shocks at once."

There was a knock at the door. Without waiting for an answer, Jan came in, his mouth full
of bread and cheese.

"Ruth, I meant to tell you I haven't got my
treasure box any more," he said. "I was so busy
rescuing Edek that I forgot all about it. I suppose it's at the bottom of the lake now."

"But the silver sword!" cried Ruth. "Is that
lost too?"

"Everything in the box is lost," said Jan, ruefully. "Now the fishes have all my treasures. As they're not secrets any more, I'll tell you what they were. Two cats' claws, a gold curtain ring, and the buttons off a German uniform. Half a pen nib and an acorn. A stick of Russian shaving soap with some hairs from Ivan's chin stuck in it. Frau Wolff's can opener. A silver teaspoon from that house in Berlin where the English soldier lived — you didn't know I'd kept that, did you, Ruth? The brightest feather in Jimpy's tail — that was precious. And three dead fleas from the hairy chest of Bistro, the chimpanzee. Bistro gave them to me himself, and I shall miss them dreadfully."

For one who had suffered so shattering a loss, he did not look as grief-stricken as you might have expected. His eyes were prouder than his words.

"But the sword?" said Ruth, who had found it hard to wait for the catalogue to end. "I gave it back to you — I know I did. I saw you put it in the box and —"

"Ah, the sword," said Jan, pulling a long face. He looked at Joseph. "If I'd lost the sword, we should never have found you again."

He bared his chest. And there, hanging from a string round his neck, was the silver sword.

He untied the sword and handed it to Ruth's mother.

"This was the most precious of all my treasures," he said. "Joseph gave it to me, but it's yours now. You can keep it forever if you'll be my mother."

CHAPTER 29

THE NEW BEGINNING

ON a bare hillside in the Swiss canton of Appenzell a village was being built. It was an international children's village, the first of its kind in the world. Before the war there was only an old farmhouse there, surrounded by fields with flocks of sheep and herds of cows with tinkling bells. Now the first house, with its broad gables and deep eaves, was already up. Others were going up at top speed. Swiss schoolchildren had collected thirty thousand pounds to help pay for the work. A great Swiss youth organization had provided more. Many of the workers gave their help free. Men and boys came from all over Europe. By 1946 Danes, Swedes, Austrians, English, Swiss, Germans, and Italians were camping together and working happily side by side. A few months before, some of them had been in opposite armies fight-

212

ing each other. Now they had joined together to build a village where abandoned and orphaned children could forget the misery of war, where their minds and bodies could be healed and they could learn to live in peace. Here at last they would find a real home, with no fear of being driven out among strangers again. They would be educated in "mind, hand, and heart." When they grew up, they would be able to meet the future with good will and courage.

These ideals made a great appeal to Joseph Balicki, who had been one of the earliest and keenest helpers. In Warsaw he had been headmaster of his own school. Now he and his wife were chosen to be the housefather and housemother of the Polish house. Each nation was to have its own house, where sixteen orphaned children could grow up with the family of the houseparents. They would be taught in their own language and join the children from the other houses for games and social activities.

Joseph had his family to help build the house, and it was one of the first to be finished. It had central heating, shower baths, electric fittings in the kitchen, bright living rooms, and gay bedrooms. The children had never known such comfort. By the late summer of 1946 they had settled in with sixteen orphaned children from Poland.

The war produced countless tragic stories, few of which ended as happily as that of the Balicki family. Yet it would be wrong to pretend that life for the Balickis was at once serene and free of trouble. They had been parted too long and suffered too much. It took time to grow used to a life which was so different from anything they had known before.

On the whole, Bronia was the quickest to settle down. She had been only four when her mother had been taken away. Too young to remember happier days, she had quickly accepted Ruth as her new mother. And through the terrible hardships of the war, Ruth had looked after her with wonderful devotion. Restored now to her parents, Bronia grew up as a happy and gifted child. Her talent for drawing matured. At first she could draw only the scenes of war and escape which she had lived through. Her pictures were full of soldiers, ruined buildings, open railway trucks, and queues outside the soup kitchens. Gradually her subjects changed. Soon they began to reflect her new and far more secure life among the mountains of Switzerland.

Edek was not so fortunate. Many of the children admitted to the village showed signs of tuberculosis. But hardship and lack of good food had made Edek much more delicate than most. He had to be sent away to a sanatorium, and for the first month or two the doctors despaired of his life. But the will to live was strong in him, and he grew better. After eighteen months he returned to his family. Another six months of open-air life in the mountains made him fit enough to go to Zürich and study engineering. He had always wanted to be an engineer.

And what of Jan, that charming bundle of good intentions and atrocious deeds? His complete record, so far as it was known, was sent to the I.T.S., but nothing came of it and his parents were never traced. So he became a Balicki. During the war his mind had suffered more than his body, and minds usually take longer to heal. He did not take easily to a secure and peaceful life. He was excitable and could not concentrate on one thing for long. He liked to play at firing squads and torture, at crossing the frontier secretly, and at smuggling. He was always fighting. Though he had all the food and clothes he needed, he was the biggest thief in the village. He broke into the other houses and raided the larders — it was usually the German house, for he still hated Germans and could not forgive them for what they had done to Poland. Margrit Balicki treated him as lovingly as she did her own children, but he was often rude to her. Ruth was the only person who could manage him, and he remained as devoted to her as ever. She knew that the way to his heart was through animals. She persuaded her father to let him keep rabbits and goats. She took him to neighboring farms, and soon the farmers found that he could do anything with a sick animal. If a cow was ill or a horse lame, they found it would get better more quickly if they sent for Jan instead of for the vet. And of course it cost them much less.

So in time even Jan grew up, and his bad ways began to drop from him. There were no more raids on larders, and the German children no longer got a shower of rotten apples at their heads whenever they passed the Polish house.

Lastly, Ruth. She had all the time been so brave, wise, and unselfish that you might have expected her to present no problem at all. But she had grown up too quickly and shouldered responsibilities far beyond her years. As she wanted to be a teacher, her father lost no time in arranging for her to go away to a university

to be trained. She refused to go. Her parents and her new home meant so much to her that she could not bring herself to leave them. She behaved like a young child, clinging to her mother and following her about everywhere. It seemed as if she were trying to recover the lost years of her childhood.

But this phase did not last long. Little by little the magic of her new surroundings worked its spell upon her. In 1947 she went to Zürich University to study for a degree. Four years later, as a qualified teacher, she married a young Frenchman who had come to work in the children's village. When a second French house was built, she and her husband were

made the houseparents. The last time I heard
of her she had sixteen French orphans under
her care, as well as two small girls of her own.
As far as I know she is there still, bringing them
up in the spirit of the children's village, giving
them all the trust and affection that young people need.

And over the way, at the Polish house, in a
velvet-lined drawer of her jewel box, Margrit
Balicki keeps her proudest possession: the silver
sword.